NOTHING PERSONAL

Heather Dentman had written love letters which fell into the wrong hands, and now she was being blackmailed. She wasn't afraid of her husband, but of her strait-laced mother-in-law Cecile, who would tighten the purse-strings if she found out. Mark Preston got the assignment, but instead of the letters, all he found was a corpse — and three tough characters from the East, who seemed to think he would also look well in the morgue.

PETER CHAMBERS

NOTHING
PERSONAL

Complete and Unabridged

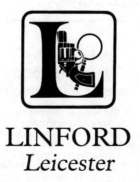

LINFORD
Leicester

First published in Great Britain in 1980

First Linford Edition
published 2005

British Library CIP Data

Chambers, Peter, *1924* –
   Nothing personal.—Large print ed.—
   Linford mystery library
   1. Preston, Mark (Fictitious character)—
   Fiction 2. Private investigators—England—
   Fiction 3. Detective and mystery stories
   4. Large type books
   I. Title
   823.9′14 [F]

   ISBN 1–84395–601–2

Published by
F. A. Thorpe (Publishing)
Anstey, Leicestershire

Set by Words & Graphics Ltd.
Anstey, Leicestershire
Printed and bound in Great Britain by
T. J. International Ltd., Padstow, Cornwall

This book is printed on acid-free paper

1

Rain, sudden, devastating, all-pervasive, drowned out the fourth race at the Palmtrees track. Paddocks became bogs, enclosures transformed into quagmires, and all in a space of minutes. I'd been under the half-shelter of a ticket window at the pari-mutuel when it broke, so I was lucky. When it stopped, quickly as it came, I stepped out into three inches of mud, drawing unfriendly glances from other racegoers who'd taken the full weight of it.

The horses I'd been intending to play in the last two races of the day would have no chance with the now-treacherous going. I'd about decided to call it quits and go home, when a voice said,

'A dry man, as I live and breathe.'

And there was Mournful Harris, as thin and cadaverous as ever. Baggy clothes, now sodden with water, wrapped around the bony frame wherever they could.

Sparse lank hair was plastered in ratstails along the sides of his sallow face. The gray rabbits-teeth bobbed about in a nervous parody of a smile.

'Oh hi, Mournful. Nice day for the racing.'

Harris is what unkind people would call a tout. He will parlay some sucker into betting a certain horse, the idea being he catches part of the action if it wins.

'Nicer than you know,' he agreed, nodding sadly. 'First the rain. Now you, dry as a bone. An omen, believe me.'

Much as I suspected I'd regret it, I asked,

'How's that? With the omen?'

He looked around, for all the world like a First Murderer, and dropped his voice.

'This meeting was a bust for me from the start. I only had one good horse, one sure-fire post-passer, but I knew it was a waste of my time. Hard turf, good going, this was no place for my horse. A mudder, you see.'

I began to see very quickly. A mudder is a nag that flourishes on the soft going.

On precisely the kind that would be waiting for the fifth and sixth races. Reluctantly, I took out my card.

'What's the name of this champion?'

'Wicked Ways. Sixth race. Wicked Ways.' He peered over my shoulder. 'See, there she is, right there.'

She was there all right. Along with a lot of background dope on her history and performance. I sighed.

'How can you do this, Mournful?' I demanded. 'The only information missing from this card is the address of the glue-factory this thing escaped from.'

'Believe me,' he whispered importantly, 'this whole thing is a clean-up operation. They been trotting this filly from one meeting to the next, just waiting for freak conditions. A man could get rich.'

Well, the day was ruined anyway, I decided. And, as any horse-player will tell you, an omen is an omen. Sticking my hand in a pocket, I came out with a fistful of crumpled bills. I counted out fifty and handed them over.

'You do it. With a thing like this, I prefer to remain anonymous. Drop the winnings into my office later.'

He stared at the money in disbelief. Mournful would normally allow at least fifteen minutes for the sell. I squelched away leaving him standing.

★ ★ ★

I stopped off at Parkside for a quick clean-up, and made it into the office a little before five p.m. Florence Digby looked surprised.

'I didn't expect you, Mr. Preston. Did somebody dynamite the track?'

'No, there's a new mob in town. They use a flooding technique. Any calls?'

'Note on your desk. I'll come in.'

I went through to my own office. Everything was immaculate, as always. And why wouldn't it be? I never do any work in there. The piece of white paper was an intrusion on the gleaming desk-top. I flopped down in the heavy leather chair and picked it up.

'Mrs. Heather Dentman,' I read aloud. 'Who's she?'

Florence parked neatly on the upright

chair opposite, disposing the trim pink skirt with care.

'Mrs. Dentman called at 2.18 this afternoon. She has a matter she would like to discuss with you. I asked if she could indicate the general nature of her business, but she said she preferred to speak with you. And face to face. Apparently she puts no trust in the telephone.'

Mrs. Dentman wasn't all fool, I decided.

'Is she going to call again?'

'It was left that you would call her. Mrs. Dentman is not the kind of person who calls more than once.'

It was hard to judge from Miss Digby's cool and measured tone just what kind of person Mrs. Dentman was.

'Well, I don't know Florence, I'm kind of busy right now — '

'Mrs. Dentman,' she bored on, unheeding, 'lives at Apartment 906, at 67 Bay Heights.'

I didn't feel so busy, suddenly. Anybody who can meet the tab in one of those millionaire blocks at the Bay end of town, is entitled to at least one phone call.

'How did she sound?'

'Like money. Old money.'

I grinned. Florence is a terrible snob. With her there are two kinds of money. There is new money, which means it belongs to somebody who worked for it, fought for it, stole it or whatever, and everybody knows how he came by it. And there is old money, which means it belongs to somebody who did nothing except to inherit from somebody else. All the fighting and stealing was long ago, and now forgotten. Old money means respectable. I never yet met anyone who cared whether he was paid in old or new money. Just so long as he gets paid.

'I meant did she sound worried, frightened, or what?'

'She wasn't hysterical, if that's what you mean. But there was — yes — strain. Strain in her voice, I would judge.'

'Did she sound as old as the money?'

I couldn't resist pulling Florence's leg. She looked miffed.

'Not old at all, I wouldn't say. Perhaps in her middle years.'

Us girls in our middle years have to stick together, her tone implied.

'If this turns out to be the one about the missing poodle, you get to pay for the call,' I threatened. 'Get her for me, will you?'

But Mrs. Heather Dentman was not to be got, as it developed. Florence tried a number of times in the next quarter hour, without result. When it came time to close up the store, I told her,

'I'll take a detour on the way home, see if the lady is receiving.'

Bay Heights is exactly what the name implies. A development along the line of the bay, and on rising ground. Away from the bustle of the seafront, with its seafront, with its ships and cranes, warehouses and docks. No smell of oil or fish up here. The commercial realities of our busy trading port are put into a more acceptable perspective, assuming almost a romantic aspect, from this safe, luxurious angle. Number Six Seven was an imposing white pile, standing well clear of its neighbors, with three fountains in front.

I walked through revolving doors into this closed world where all was quiet and cool. Maybe the black marble floor helped to keep down the temperature. Certainly there was nothing warm about the inspection I was getting from the man in the alpaca suit who watched me from a desk marked 'Manager'. He was fifty years old, with a wise, rumpled face, and a hard look around the eyes which was all too familiar. The denizens of number six seven could call him the manager all they wanted, but to me, everything about him yelled cop.

'Evening,' I nodded. 'I'm calling on 906. A Mrs. Heather Dentman.'

'I don't believe I've seen you before, sir.' The 'sir' came out with a reluctant, grating sound. 'What name would it be?'

'Preston.' I showed him the buzzer. 'She's half-expecting me.'

He looked at my I.D. with great care. Most people just see the photograph, and the stamp where it says 'State of California'. This guy wasn't most people. He checked the date, everything.

'This must be a pleasant change from

8

the old precinct house, right?' I ventured.

That brought me a fair imitation of a grin.

'It still shows, huh? Well, I was with the department eighteen years. I guess a man don't shrug that off too easy. Preston. Something about the name.'

I mentioned one or two police officers I'd worked with, and soon hit one he'd known, and right off we were gabbing away about things which would have been very enlightening to his new employers.

' — and when I got out of the hospital, they told me one of the slugs had loused up this leg of mine, and I'd always have a limp. I'd have to leave the force, you see. But the commissioner looks after his own. Wasn't long before he got me fixed up with this job.'

'He'd probably prefer to have an honest copper doing this kind of work than some of these mushroom security firms,' I suggested.

'Right,' he agreed. 'Name is Hackett, by the way. Two 'T's'.'

We shook hands. I picked up my picture and stuck it in my pocket.

'You wouldn't want a copy of the mug-shot?' I offered. 'Just for security reasons.'

'No need,' he told me. 'I already have a moving picture of you. You, and everybody else who comes through those doors. These people are paying top money for protection. They get it. I'll call up 906.'

He picked up a green telephone, and pushed buttons. After a wait, he muttered into it, nodded, and replaced the receiver.

'Lady says to go up.'

'Thanks. I've never actually met her. What kind of a lady is she?'

His face was a mask again.

'Old times is old times,' he said flatly. 'These are new times. I don't get paid to gossip about my people. Just to protect 'em, is all.'

'O.K. I'll see you, Hackett.'

The elevator was one of these hi-speed, no motion affairs. The doors seemed scarcely to have closed in front of me, before a mellow bell went 'ping' and a red light glowed over the figure 9. I stepped out into carpeted silence. On the wall opposite the elevator, a board with an arrow announced that 906–910 were to the right. At 906, I leaned on the buzzer, and stood back from the door. At these prices, there was certain to be some way the person inside could scrutinise the person outside before deciding to open up.

The door opened soundlessly. There was nobody on the other side. A voice said from above the door,

'Please come in, Mr. Preston.'

I went in, and behind me the door closed as silently as it opened. The room I was standing in was huge, richly-carpeted, and furnished in a style vaguely Oriental. By a vast, curving window some twenty feet away, a woman inspected me with interest.

'So you're Mark Preston.'

'Good evening, Mrs. Dentman.'

I was inspecting her with interest, too, and getting the better of the deal. She was thirty plus, black hair swept up from the pale oval face, accentuating the redness of her mouth against sparkling teeth. Tallish, maybe five seven, slender without being angular, with a high-collar soft wool dress in pale green. Not to waste any time with poetry, Mrs. Dentman was a knockout.

'The way you spoke just then,' I began, 'sounded as though the name is familiar?'

'Yes.' She rubbed a hand down her arm, in a quick, nervous movement. 'Julia mentioned you to me. Julia Redbourne.'[1]

That one. I remembered her, and with pleasure. They would have looked well together, those two. But I didn't say that. What I said was,

'Ah, yes. How is Mrs. Redbourne?'

'I haven't seen her in months. But she seemed to think very highly of you. So when this cropped up, I thought of you straight off.'

I nodded encouragingly. The first conversation is always the worst. People will talk about anything except the matter in hand. Politics, the weather, anything. There was a man one time spent ten clear minutes describing what he'd had for breakfast that day. All I had to do was listen. Eventually they all had to come

[1] The Deader They Fall.

around to it. 'This', after all, had cropped up. And I was going to have to be told what 'this' was.

'Would you like anything? A drink, perhaps?'

Another stall.

'Thank you, that would be fine. A very little Scotch, and a lot of water.'

That gave her something to do. She could move around, selecting glasses, fiddling with bottles. And as long as she was moving around, that gave me something to do as well. I could look at her.

'Is that all right?'

She held out a chunky glass half-filled with the pale amber liquid.

'It looks just fine. Thank you. Aren't you having one?'

'Um? Oh. Well, yes, perhaps. Yes, a small something.'

Slender brown fingers clamped around a square gin-bottle. She poured out about enough to drown the average housefly, then added four inches of tonic water. Heather Dentman was evidently nobody's idea of a hard drinker.

'Julia said you were easy to talk to,' she accused.

'Well, I don't growl or anything,' I replied.

'Then why can't I talk to you?'

'Maybe it's connected with the subject matter.'

'Maybe.'

She turned away from me, staring out the window again.

'That rain was awful, wasn't it?'

'Terrible.'

'So unexpected.'

'Very.'

'I want to talk about blackmail.'

'I'm still here.'

She looked back at me then. She wasn't the type to blush, but there was a kind of shyness on her face. A look of being almost defenseless. It was very appealing, and a weapon which would be the equivalent to dynamite in a boy and girl situation. Which this wasn't, I reminded myself.

I winked at her.

'There you are. That scarcely hurt at all, did it? Tell me about the blackmail.'

'I have an odd kind of marriage, Mr. Preston. My husband and I live together, in a ramshackle kind of way. But there's nothing there. Nothing solid. We lead our own lives, without being too untidy about it, if you understand me.'

Untidy. Nice word. I wondered what it meant.

'You mean you try to behave discreetly, in your — um — separate lives.'

'Just so. I probably take care rather more than George does, but then, a woman has to, doesn't she?'

She said it without rancour, and I knew what she meant. People were quite willing to support campaigns, write articles and so forth, all in the name of women's liberation. At the same time, they didn't expect women to get too liberal. As the saying goes, it's not the same for a man.

'I guess she does,' I said, non-committally.

'I met this man. Some months ago, now. It didn't seem anything special at first, then I found I was getting involved. I started to feel like a young girl again. I even wrote him notes, the way a girl would. You don't have to tell me how foolish it was. I even knew it was at the time, but I couldn't help it, somehow.'

I sipped at my colored water.

'Am I allowed to ask his name?'

'Clive Barnes. He's the tennis professional at Bay End Club. You may know the name.'

She was speaking more easily now. They usually do, once they get started. I'd heard it all before, anyway. This was Classic Case Number Five. The Lady and the Tennis Bum. It went way back.

'I may have heard it,' I conceded. 'Forest Hills, perhaps?'

She nodded vigorously.

'Oh yes, all the major tournaments. He's very good, you know.'

'Tell me about the letters,' I prodded.

The momentary animation on her face vanished as fast as it had come.

'The other day, Clive was away. Playing down in San Diego. While he was gone, his apartment was burgled. Nothing seemed to be missing at first, and he couldn't make sense of it. Then, a few days ago, I had a telephone call. It was a man. He said he had the letters I'd written to Clive. I could have them back for twenty thousand dollars.'

'Was the voice familiar?'

'No. But it was muffled, somehow. As though he were speaking through a bad microphone.'

I wondered how old Clive would sound, through two layers of handkerchief.

'So, your instructions are to get hold of this money, in used, unmarked bills, and await a further call.'

A look of faint surprise came over the pale features.

'Almost word perfect,' she confirmed. 'This would seem to be an old story, to you.'

'Let's just say it isn't entirely unfamiliar. You've talked to this man Barnes about it, of course.'

That brought the ghost of a smile.

'Oh, yes. His reaction was typical. He wanted me to follow out what this man said, to the letter. The only difference would be that wherever the money went, he would be right behind it. He would then personally tear this man, or men, limb from limb, recover the money and the letters, and that would be the end of the matter.'

I could believe one part of it. The part where old Clive said he would be right behind the money.

'That sounds like a good, male reaction,' I suggested. 'But you didn't think much of it?'

'Not much,' she agreed. 'It's all very well being strong and brave, and so forth, but this isn't that kind of situation. These people are criminals. They are not going to stand up in the open and indulge in fisticuffs. Alley-rats most likely. With guns, I shouldn't be surprised. Much as I love him, I don't think Clive really understands what he would be up against. He might even get himself killed.'

'That's very good thinking, Mrs. Dentman.' I meant it. 'And so you thought you'd be better with someone like me. You did the right thing, calling me. But I must warn you, these blackmail cases can be the very devil. I might need an assistant, even two. I can only be one place at a time, and some of these instructions get very complicated.'

'I understand that. Will you act for me?'

'Consider me hired. First off, what about the police?'

Alarm now.

'Police?' she repeated.

'Sure. The burglary of Barnes' apartment. Did they come up with anything? Any ideas?'

A little color came back into her face.

'Oh, I see. No. That is, they weren't involved.'

Surprise, surprise. I tried to look surprised.

'Not involved?'

'Well no. There was no point, you see. So far as he could tell, Clive that is, nothing had been taken. Once he sat and thought about it, he decided there was no reason to call the police. He would have to answer a lot of questions, and his first thought was the need for me to be protected.'

Naturally. Good old Clive.

'Yes, I see that. Now, the practical

details. Can you lay hands on this kind of money, Mrs. Dentman? Without attracting any attention, I mean.'

'I've done nothing about it, as yet. You see the fact is, I'm not a wealthy woman, despite all the trappings here. What money there is, is my husband's.'

That gave me pause. I would have thought even a tennis jerk would have looked into the practicalities.

'Are you saying you can't raise the money?'

'Not without bringing George into this. I haven't told him anything, so far.'

Things which had been clear one minute earlier suddenly became clouded over. I frowned.

'Sometimes I don't think too clearly in the early evening,' I began. 'Could we just run over this again? You have written some letters, and these have got into the wrong hands. You are required to pay for their recovery. The only way you can meet the tab is to ask your husband for the money. Forgive me, if I'm not making sense of this. Maybe I left something out. The way it stacks up, you now have to say to your husband, 'George, please let me have twenty thousand dollars so I can buy back some letters you mustn't know I wrote'. Tell me where I went wrong.'

She had been listening attentively. Now the gleaming black hair bobbed up and down.

'Yes, I see exactly. And it isn't your fault. It's mine, for not explaining things properly. I'm not all that concerned about George being mixed up in this. He'll be angry, of course, and if it were possible to leave him out, then I would do so.'

'But where does the blackmail angle come in? I mean, if you're going to tell your husband anyway — '

'It's not my husband we're concerned with. The letters will be sent to my mother-in-law. To George's mother.'

'Ah.'

Well, it was a beginning. There'd have to be more, lots more. But at least it proved I wasn't cracking up.

'Let me explain a little about our marriage. It's the old American story. I'm the one with the breeding, so-called, George is the one with the money. Or, more precisely, his mother is. Cecile Dentman is a very formidable lady who is not interested in the permissive society. The sanctity of marriage is the same now as it was at the turn of the century, so far as she is concerned. She's a wonderful woman in many ways, generous to a fault. But she has always made it entirely clear that she will tolerate no form of scandal. One whiff of it, and this applies even more stringently to me than to my dear husband, and there will be no more money. Not now. Not ever. Don't let me give you the wrong impression. Cecile is not your traditional purse-holder, shelling out a few dollars with reluctance every now and then. The money is available, and freely. But on this one point, she is quite adamant. I have to be above reproach. Now, do you understand?'

I began to feel sympathy for the unknown Cecile. And with it, less for my new client. It seemed to me, with a set-up like she obviously had, Heather Dentman was not giving value for money. Something must have showed on my face.

'You haven't much of an opinion of me, have you?'

The tone was slightly bitter, the eyes anxious.

'Mrs. Dentman,' I said without emphasis, 'I'm a private investigator. That's the way I hire out, and that's what I do. I'm not in the business of judgement, that's for courtrooms. My concern here is to get those letters back. I think, for the moment, you'd do well to leave your husband out of this. If we can resolve the problem without his knowledge, I'm sure it would be better all round. Do you agree?'

'If it's possible, yes. Yes, of course. What are you going to do?'

'Well, there isn't much to go on, until our mysterious caller gets back to you. I'll start off by going to see Clive Barnes. Tell him you've brought me into this, let him see what I look like. Wouldn't do if we were strangers. If he decides to hawkshaw around on this thing, he might even think I'm the blackmailer, and start putting the slug on me. If you'd let me have his address please.'

I wrote it down, and got ready to leave. At the door, I turned to her and said,

'We must understand each other. From now on, I have to be in control of this. Every aspect. Whatever you do, don't go making any moves of your own. You're going to have to trust me, Mrs. Dentman.'

She nodded gravely.

'I'd already decided that, before I called your office. Now that I've talked with you, I'm quite happy about it.'

'If you can't get me at any time, call me at home. The number is on the card.'

'Good luck.'

In this racket, luck is one part good fortune and nine parts shoe leather.

I pointed my shoes towards the elevator.

2

It looked like being one of the shortest cases on record. All I had to do was go along and bang on Clive Barnes' door. We would have a little chat about philosophy, and what a strange old world this is, and love, true, the course of. I would contribute a bit about how much I admired the game of tennis, and never missed any TV coverage of the major events. I would commisserate with him about those future close-in shots of himself on the courts, and how unfeeling it was of the cameramen to concentrate on his face, now that all those front teeth were missing. He would probably agree that all right-thinking citizens should do all they could to prevent the screening of shots like that. I would then explain my little scheme for getting the better of the cameramen. We would argue back and forth a while about the details. Finally he would make a choice. He could keep either the teeth or the letters, but not both. All that would remain would be for me to give Heather Dentman back her little blue-ribboned package, charge my minimum three-day fee, and take the following day off. A man should be careful not to overwork himself in this day and age.

Between the tennis and the occasional offhand blackmail, Clive Barnes seemed to be doing very well. The address I had led me to a pleasant tree-shaded avenue, with neat bungalows either side of a wide road. There was a new black Caddy parked in the block top drive-way, and a red Toyota sedan sitting out front, facing sideways. Someone had the small front yard under good control. I reached out a hand towards the glove compartment where the .38 was stashed, then changed my mind and left it. He might come on strong like a good athlete, but as his lady-love had said herself, this was alley work. Evening shadows were lengthening rapidly across the wooden porch as I pressed the bell.

Almost at once, the door opened. A

whole inch. I couldn't see much more than an eye.

'What do you want?'

The voice was low and gritty.

'Like to have a talk with you, Barnes.'

'Who are you?'

'The name is Preston. We could talk better inside. Or you could come out here, if you prefer.'

'Go away.'

The door began to close, but I already had a foot there.

'Don't be hard to live with,' I begged. 'You're going to talk to me, whether you want to or not.'

A pause. Then,

'You better come in.'

The door swung inwards, I stepped in quickly before he changed his mind.

'Through here.'

He was shorter than I'd expected. I followed him into the house and a wide lounging room. He turned suddenly, sank a fist like a steam hammer into my middle, and slammed me against the wall. There was cold metal, round and unfeeling against my windpipe.

'What the — ?' I muttered, feebly.

'Shuddup.'

Hard fingers jabbed at me, searching around. It all happened so fast that only now was I getting a look at the man who slugged me. His face was swarthy, and he'd been carrying it around for thirty years. The olive eyes, the gritty voice, and the gun, made me wonder whether I had the right man. And those hands had searched for a weapon before.

Satisfied, he stood clear of me. Well clear.

'He's clean,' he announced.

'Then let's not keep him waiting.'

I looked towards the direction of the new voice. At the far side of the room, two other men stood, watching our little love-play at the door. The one who'd spoken was the shorter of the two. Medium height, with a heavy-jowled blueshave complexion and a heavy red mouth. Thick black hair was brushed away over his ears beneath a white panama hat. The gray silk suit hung on his thick frame the way three hundred dollars worth is supposed to.

His companion was an inch taller, with curly brown hair above a chirpy, grinning face. Eager, like a puppy dog. A conservative dresser, this one. Black shirt, no tie, a yellow windcheater and tartan pants. The heavy brogue shoes were black and white.

My new friend with the gun motioned me to go further into the room. Puzzled, I went ahead of him, and we all stood looking at each other.

'Which of you is Barnes?' I demanded. 'And just what — '

'Shuddup.'

A prod from the gun emphasised the point.

'Shortie is right. When you come busting into a man's house you oughta be more polite.'

This from the obvious leader of this ill-assorted trio. For some reason, although they were in complete control of the situation, they weren't at ease.

'Now, let's have it. Who are you, and what do you want here?'

'Name is Preston, as I said before. And I came to talk with Clive Barnes.'

The boss-man nodded.

'Never seen you before. Suppose I told you I was Barnes?'

'Then I'd have to come clean. I'm really Popeye the Sailor.'

The one with the chirpy face let out a short barking laugh of delight. It lit up his eyes. The other two just stared at him, and he stopped as fast as he started.

'A tough guy,' scoffed my escort. 'Let me kind of bat him round the head a little bit.'

I was beginning to get mad, which is never a smart idea when you're up against three solid churchgoers like these mugs.

'You come near me with that thing,' I told him nastily, 'and you better shoot it off. If you don't I'll wrap it round your throat.'

'Why — '

'Shortie. Take it easy.' The man in the white hat was puzzled. 'You talk a big game, Preston. Maybe you've seen a gun before?'

'Maybe. They're for shooting people. Otherwise, they're just lumps of metal. You guys don't have any reason to shoot

30

me. So shove the gun. And tell me what this is all about.'

His face relaxed a little, as some of the watchfulness went out of it.

'What do you want to see Barnes about?'

'Personal. It has to do with a lady. Her name is no concern of yours.'

'A dame?' Chirpy-face spoke for the first time. 'Say, that would — '

'Can it,' ordered his boss. 'Well, if it's just a personal thing, I guess there's no reason you shouldn't see him. He's in there. Kind of hiding, you might say.'

An enormous thumb jerked towards a door at the far end of the room. I looked over, uncertain.

'Go ahead. It's O.K.'

I walked to the door he'd pointed out, a feeling of growing unease inside me. The door was slightly ajar, so I pushed it open.

'Barnes?'

It was a bedroom, and seemed to be empty. After a final look round at the three watching men, I stepped inside.

'You in here, Barnes?'

Heavy curtains had been pulled across the windows, making it difficult to see. I walked over to draw them open, and stumbled over something. The something was a foot. At the other end of it was the rest of a man.

In that moment, I knew two things. The man was going to be Clive Barnes. And Barnes was going to be dead. He'd fallen on his face, and there was no sign of a wound on his back. Grunting at having to shift the dead weight, I pulled him round, and saw dark stains on the white shirtfront. In that light there was no telling whether they'd been caused by a knife or a gun. I stood up, letting the body fall back into position. This was one hell of a development, I decided. I'd elected him for the blackmail spot, but with him being dead, that no longer seemed so certain. If we'd been alone I could have turned the place over, looking for the letters. But we were not alone. There were three characters in the next room who may or may not have bumped off the Bay End Club tennis pro. If they had, it would seem to me no more than plain common sense that they would hit me into the bargain. It was a question of simple insurance. Even if they hadn't, it would be foolish for me to let them know the letters existed. They might decide to do a little offhand blackmailing on their own account. Never turn away a soft dollar, that's a rule where those guys came from. I was standing there, trying to resist the impulse to search through the furniture, when a voice said,

'Hey, you through talking with the pretty boy?'

Chirpy-face stood in the doorway, staring in.

Maybe I could rush him, use him as a shield to get me past the others. Maybe there'd be a gun in his pocket and we could go in for a little table-turning. Maybe nothing. It wasn't his first day out of school. He stood well back from the door, and said,

'C'mon out. You've seen him.'

I went back outside to where the others waited.

'Lost some of his bounce, didn't he?'

This from the boss-man, who watched me impassively.

'I would say he's all bounced out,' I replied evenly. 'It didn't look like heart failure.'

'Guy like that, it was a cinch somebody would get to him, sooner or later,' he shrugged. 'We been having a meeting here. The thing is, what do we do with you?'

Well, at least I wasn't going to join Barnes that very minute.

'I say we knock him off.'

Shortie accompanied his contribution with a savage downward thumb movement. I could learn to dislike Shortie, I decided. Walking a couple of yards further into the room, I parked in a chair, and pulled out my Old Favorites.

'My old daddy used to say you ought to count ten before you bump anybody off.'

It was a relief to see the lighter-flame held steady. Chirpy-face brayed his staccato laugh again.

'Style,' he chuckled. 'There ain't so much of it around any more. And maybe he's right, at that. You ought to have a reason to knock a man off.'

'A reason,' exploded Shortie. 'A reason? Here we got this stiff right here in the house. We got this Preston, who can put the finger on the whole lot of us. This ain't a reason?'

'He's got a point there, Preston. Whaddya say?' queried the leader.

It isn't every day a man gets to chip in with a view about his own execution. Like somebody once said, it concentrates the mind.

'My vote is no,' I announced. 'What do we have here? A bunch of people, all strangers to me. One of them is dead. So? People die every day. It's none of my business. And I'm a man who keeps himself to himself.'

'You mean you wouldn't go running to the cops?' demanded the boss-man.

'Why would I want to do that? Barnes is nothing to me. I don't even know who you people are. And don't forget your hole-card.'

I left it hanging around, so somebody could grab at it, turn it into a question.

'What's this hole-card?' queried Chirpy-face.

I grinned at him thankfully.

'You can locate me any time you like. I'd be lying if I said I wasn't well known in this town. Even if the cops did latch onto me, turn me into some kind of witness, I'd never make it to the stand.'

'That's sense,' decided my questioner. Turning to the others, he said, 'That's sense, ain't it? We could knock him off any time. I vote we leave it till we have to.'

Shortie mumbled something I didn't hear, and scowled at the ceiling. Chirpy-face nodded.

'You got it, boss. He ain't going no place.'

I sat there smoking, and trying to keep anxiety from my face. It isn't easy when the execution squad is holding a meeting. And all this talk about votes was strictly for the birds. The boss wasn't really paying any attention to anything his outriders were saying. He was just letting them prattle on while he got his own thinking straight. At the end he would make his own decision, yes or no, and the

36

others would do as he said. When I come to list my ten most enjoyable experiences, this one I would leave out.

'O.K.,' he decided. 'Today you got lucky, Preston. The guy who was chasing your girl-friend got himself scragged. Be grateful for it. You caught me in a soft mood. But you start playing footsie with the coppers, and you're dead. You listening to me?'

'I'm listening. And don't worry.'

He came and stuck his face close to mine. He stank of old cigar smoke and stale face lotion.

'I never worry,' he emphasised. 'I ain't the worrying kind. You get out of line, and I'll kill you. It won't worry me a bit. You'd better believe it.'

I believed it.

Without looking round, he jerked his head and walked towards the door. The others followed. Shortie wouldn't look at me. The man with the bright eyes winked cheerfully as he followed the others. He didn't fool me with all that good-guy routine. He'd have rubbed me out just like swatting a fly if that had been the decision.

They trooped out, leaving the door open. Still uncertain, and knowing I wouldn't be satisfied until I saw them out of sight, I crossed to the window, looking out. Shortie was whispering excitedly into the leader's ear, and not getting much by way of response. Chirpy-face opened the door of the Caddy. I noted the licence plate. From that position I couldn't do the same with the Toyota.

I was straining every nerve to overhear what was being said, and not making any progress. My faculties were all directed out there, which must have explained why I didn't hear any other sound. At that moment, something slammed against the side of my head. The scene exploded into a thousand bright fragments, followed by swift enveloping darkness. The second blow was no more than a dull pat at my skull as my knees hit the deck. The floorboards were scrubbed and polished pine as I stretched out on them.

★   ★   ★

When I opened one eye, there was darkness. I seemed to be lying on something hard, and wondered vaguely why that should be. My head ached and my mouth felt like the day after Christmas. I was going to have to be more careful what I drank. The party must have been a wow, I decided, because I couldn't remember it at all. Time to get up. The movement brought jolting pain between my ears, and I put up a hand in a reflex action. There was a lump on the back of my head, and I couldn't remember that either. I seemed to be lying on somebody's floor, though it was too dark to make out any detail. I'd made it as far as my knees when I remembered who owned the floor. I stayed in that crouched position for two whole minutes, gathering my strength and my wits at the same time. When I finally stood upright, things were more or less clear in my mind. I'd been watching the three thugs leaving the Barnes house, and somebody slugged me from behind. There'd been a fourth man the whole time, and I hadn't known it. For some reason, it had been important I shouldn't see his face. He'd kept out of the way while the other three went through their act, but when it came time to go home, it was sleepy-time for Preston. I tried to blame myself for not thinking of it before, but without much conviction. Three mugs at one time was quite enough to be going on with. Why should there be a fourth? Why not a fifth, or a tenth? No, I'd been outsmarted, and that was all.

What interested me was that he kept himself hidden. That made him somebody whose face I might recognise. Some well-known mobster. Or, wait a minute. Maybe not. Maybe quite the reverse. Some well-known citizen who had no racket connections at all. Somebody who would not normally be found in the kind of company he was keeping that day. Whichever answer was the right one, I'd certainly been fooled.

It was pitch dark outside. The sensible thing to do would be to get out before I was discovered in the house with a dead man. But I couldn't do the sensible thing. What had brought me here had been

Heather Dentman's letters. I would have to be satisfied they weren't around before I left. If the police found stuff like that in the same place with a corpse, the balloon would go up for my client.

It was after ten o'clock, and I'd been resting for several hours. The lights would have to be risked, because there was no way I could search a strange house in the dark. Everything looked as it had been before, as I began to poke around.

Twenty minutes later, I knew two things. Clive Barnes was just as dead as ever, and the blackmail letters were not in the house. It was an eerie experience, having to keep stepping over the dead man as I searched the bedroom, and I was relieved when the job was done. I didn't learn much about him, except he had a book of press clippings a foot thick, plus around one hundred photographs of himself with all kinds of celebrities, usually in tennis scenes. I didn't envy the police if they had to look for suspects among that bunch. His other papers didn't tell me much, except that he seemed to pay his bills punctually. There was one letter, from a sister with a Sacramento address. Otherwise it would seem the late Clive Barnes led a well-ordered life.

When I'd searched everywhere, I turned off all the lights and went outside onto the porch. Both cars were gone. I would have liked to check in the Barnes garage, but the door was one of the up-and-over variety, and I couldn't risk the noise. A lighted garage is too much like a television screen from outside. Anybody passing would be able to see me clearly, and that was no part of my plans. Inside the house, the telephone began to shrill. My head was still complaining when I climbed into the Chev and drove off.

3

I got back to Parkside, and dunked my sore head in cold water. Anytime you get into an argument with a sandbag or a length of piping, don't forget the old Doc Preston remedy. First, you immerse the affected part in six inches of cold tapwater. Dry gently, using a patting motion, and not rubbing. Next, you take a fifth of scotch. Measure four fingers carefully into a glass. Put the glass on some suitable flat surface in case it's needed for a visitor. Next, tip the bottle down your throat until a warm glow is experienced. Then, light an Old Favorite and inhale deeply. Repeat the warm glow until the aching recedes.

The remedy was beginning to work when the telephone began its unholy chatter. It was almost eleven, and I was tempted not to answer, but curiosity usually wins. Besides, it could be the Black Stallion show, and maybe I'd won a

43

year's free supply of horse-feed.

'Well?' I growled.

A man's voice answered, pleasant, well modulated, but somehow urgent.

'Preston? Mark Preston?'

'Who is this?' I countered.

'Like to talk with you a minute.'

'So talk. But first, tell me who you are.'

'I'm a man who wants to talk to you. But not on the telephone. What do you say we meet for a drink? Eleven-thirty suit you?'

My head said no. My voice said,

'Cut out all the mystery. My mother told me not to go meeting strange men at this time of night.'

He chuckled, but not pleasantly.

'What would your mother have said about you calling on a certain lady a few hours ago? Now then, about that drink.'

The only lady I'd called on that day was Heather Dentman. The guy began to interest me.

'This had better be good,' I warned him. 'Where do we do all this drinking?'

'You know Annie's Place?'

'Yes.'

'See you there.'

'Wait a minute,' I stalled. 'How will I know you?'

'Don't worry about it. I'll know you.'

He hung up. I looked at the receiver, but it had nothing to add. Thoughtfully, I replaced it. Well, if I was going out, I'd better find some clothes I hadn't been sleeping in.

Annie's place is just a five minute drive from where I live. At least, it is at that time of night. In daytime traffic, it would be a nerve-stretching twenty minutes. The joint was owned, managed and entertained by the singer, Annie Domino. She's been around since the revival of the big bands in the sixties, when her warm ebullient style soon began to push her away from the traditional confines of the orchestrations. The singer was intended to be part of the arrangement, like the brass and the reeds, and the rest of the band. Just now and then, a singer would come along who couldn't be contained within that rigid framework. When that happens, it means one of two things. Either the singer gets fired, or his name goes above the band. Or her name. Before long, it was Annie Domino, with the Big Big Band. Soon it was just Annie Domino, and that was all the customers really wanted. She was big and black and beautiful, with a voice that could bring you to your feet, yelling, one minute, and have you curled up in a ball with warm velvet rubbing down your spine the next. She grew tired of the big arenas, and the one-night stands, and as soon as she could afford it, she quit the scene. All she really wanted was her very own place, where she could relax and make her own special music when she felt like it, for a few dozen people instead of a dozen thousand. And so, Annie's Place. She'd never known her real name. Whoever left her at the orphanage also left a battered suitcase with the initials A.D. Some joker thought it referred to Anno Domini, and somehow over the years, the vowels got switched around.

I hadn't seen her in months, and as I walked through the black glass door, a little honey-colored number smiled brightly.

46

'Good evening, sir. Have you a reservation?'

She was cute. Small and dainty, with brilliant teeth and a mischievous look around the eyes. A miniature almost, with a friendly vulnerability that made you want to pop her into a pocket and take her home. To grin at this one involved no effort whatever.

'Always, honey. I always have a reservation.'

It was true. I'd been able to help Annie out one time, with a little difficulty she was having with some protection mugs. This was one door that would always be open. But Pint-Size was new.

'I'm sorry. I don't recall — '

'Sure you don't,' I soothed. 'You're new here. I go way back. The name is Preston. Now, you do whatever you're expected to do. I'll go and get a drink.'

She smiled uncertainly as I went past her into the club. The place had been done over again since I was last in. The habit of years of changing scenes had followed Annie into her permanent place. She no longer had different towns, different platforms, so she simply changed the look of the place where she was. We were all deep purple and silver this week, with imitation stars twinkling from a velvet ceiling.

I leaned against the padded leather of the bar, shaking my head in reply to the enquiring glance from the immaculate man making polishing movements with a glass. A voice said,

'Janie was right. You really are a stranger.'

The voice was pure gravel, and sounded appropriate coming from the huge man who stood beside me. He was six and one half feet tall, two hundred twenty pounds of solid muscle, and built along the general lines of a gravel-crusher. In his fighting days, Beef Bronowitz had been billed as the White Gorilla, and nobody ever queried the description.

'Hi Beef,' I greeted. 'How've you been? And who's Janie?'

'How I been is lonely. You don't come and see us no more. And Janie is the little girl outside.'

'That one. Nice. Like a pretty doll. Thought I might collect her on the way home.'

His face split into a delighted grin.

'Go ahead and try it. What you'll collect is a busted spine. That little item is a black belt plus. Did you come to drink, or to listen? Annie goes on in about an hour.'

'Came to meet a man,' I told him.

'Well, have fun,' he nodded, and went away.

I stuck a pretzel in my mouth and looked around the place. It was hard to see more than a dozen feet, because Annie doesn't believe in too much illumination. But most of what light there was came from the bar, so I should be clearly visible if someone was watching for me. After two or three minutes, a man emerged from the smoke-heavy gloom, and came towards me.

He was thirty years old, with unruly fair hair above a face which was handsome and weak at the same time. Tall and slender, he wore the expensive suit in a way that said he had plenty more where it came from. We stood and looked at each other.

'Glad you made it.' The voice was the same one I'd heard on the telephone. He didn't offer to shake hands. 'Shall we sit down? I have a table over here.'

I shrugged, and followed. Sit, stand, it made no difference to me. The table was small, and wedged against a wall. Ideal if you were with a lady, and wanted to be cosy. Or a man you wanted to talk with in private.

There was an empty glass in front of me. The fair man picked up a bottle of wine which was about one-third empty.

'Try some of this,' he suggested. 'It's very light, not too sweet.'

By way of acceptance, I moved the glass an inch towards him.

'Well, here's to it,' he announced.

I took a sip at the pale red wine, and he was right. It was light. Practically non-alcoholic, at a guess.

'Now then, Preston, what's this all about?'

I stared at him, with surprise that was not faked.

'That's rich,' I replied. 'I only came here to ask you that same question.'

He nodded, rolling the long-stemmed glass around with well-manicured fingers.

'You act as though you don't know who I am,' he accused.

'You got it,' I confirmed. 'A good place to start. Who am you?'

Now he was puzzled.

'I don't get it,' he confessed. 'You mean you don't even have any pictures of me?'

'Why would I need them? What are you, some kind of movie star or something?'

He shook his head, and stared at me intently.

'I'm George Dentman,' he announced.

'So you're George Dentman,' I repeated. 'It still doesn't tell me what you want to talk about.'

'Money. Let's talk about money.'

A man who wants to talk about money is always sure of a good audience when I'm around.

'I'm still here.'

'Listen, Preston, I've asked a couple of people about you. People who know

51

things. They say you're very good. You are also very expensive.'

I made no reply, but took another light sip at the wine.

'Whatever Heather is paying you, I will double. Now. Here.'

'What would I have to do?' I asked mildly.

'Do?' he queried, with a sudden sharp note in his voice. 'Do? Why nothing, naturally. You drop the whole thing. Forget it. Just pick up your money and blow. Find a blonde, go away for a few days. What do I care what you do?'

It seemed to me he was losing the thread of his own argument.

'You seem to care enough to give me a lot of money,' I pointed out. 'To drop whatever it is I'm supposed to be doing. What might that be, by the way? I wouldn't want to take your money under false pretenses.'

He let out a snort of exasperation. The signs were, he was beginning to lose his temper. I get extra careful around guys who blow their cool at midnight in quiet corners. And especially guys who have their fingers wrapped around a bottle.

In an attempt to calm him down, I kept my voice deliberately flat.

'Look, Mr. Dentman, don't misunderstand me. I'm not trying to rile you. It's just that I don't know what you're talking about. Why don't we start over?'

There was one obvious answer to his behaviour. Somebody had murdered Heather Dentman's boyfriend. Then somebody who didn't want to be seen, had slugged me from behind. From out of the clear night sky Heather Dentman's husband was offering me money to take a vacation. A man didn't have to be Hawkshaw the Great to string those little items into some kind of a whole.

And I was wishing he'd relax his grasp on that bottle. But when he replied, his voice was more even, more controlled.

'So we have to play charades. Very well. You called to see my wife this afternoon. Do you deny it?'

I made no reply.

'Well, it doesn't matter a damn whether you do or not. It can be proved.'

'Is that what she says?'

'She won't talk to me. Won't even answer the phone. We have this great relationship, as she probably told you. Sometimes we don't even see one another for days at a stretch. But you were there. I saw you. Our security man has a film of you coming into the place.'

Hackett. Of course. He'd told me his employers had first claim on his loyalty. George Dentman must have a standing instruction to be given information on all his wife's callers.

'All right, so I was there,' I conceded.

'Damn right, you were there. You didn't go to talk about the weather. And you didn't go to rumple any cushions, either.'

That must have brought a reaction to my hitherto expressionless face. After all, a man doesn't care to be dismissed in the cushion-rumpling league. Dentman gave a quick snorting laugh.

'Don't look so offended. It's just that I know Heather. She's not an unfaithful type, and she already has a boyfriend. It's true I don't know who he is, but I know it isn't you. That's the real reason she hired you, you know.'

He was talking in riddles again.

'You're going too fast again,' I hedged. 'Tell me about this real reason.'

He clucked with impatience.

'This divorce nonsense. It isn't because she really gives a damn what I do, where I sleep. She probably fed you some high-toned nonsense about her offended morality or dignity, or some such claptrap. But the truth is, she wants to be rid of me so she'll be free to marry the pretty boy. So there you have it. I double your pay, and you drop it. A simple matter of business. What do you say?'

I didn't know what to say. I could understand why her husband would assume Heather Dentman was hiring me on a divorce matter. But it didn't jell with her own story about the way his mother would react to the morality of it all. A divorce was certainly an improvement on a messy case of blackmail, but if old ma-in-law was as strict as Heather had indicated, it would still be an unaccept-able situation. The two things seemed to be incompatible. Which would mean somebody wasn't telling me the truth.

55

Which would, I sighed inwardly, be about normal in a case of this kind.

'Well?' snapped her husband.

'Tell you what I'll do, Mr. Dentman,' I stalled. 'I'll sleep on it. Give you an answer by noon tomorrow. And between now and then, I will undertake to do nothing whatever in the matter of any divorce proceedings.'

He didn't like it, but at least it was better than nothing.

'You're going to hold out for more money,' he accused. 'How do I know you won't contact Heather, and get some kind of an auction started?'

It was a fair question. And it would be no kind of reply for me to take a high moral tone about integrity and so forth. A man who is considering selling out his employer can't expect too high a rating in the integrity league.

'Everything O.K., gents?'

The vast frame of Beef Bronowitz suddenly blotted out such light as we'd been getting. He stood there, beaming affably down on the midgets, your genial host in person. Before I could answer,

George Dentman said,

'Sure Beef, certainly. How've you been?'

'Fine, Mr. Dentman, just fine.' Then to me, 'Why didn't you tell me it was Mr. Dentman you were looking for? I never knew you two gents were acquainted.'

'Never thought about it, Beef,' I grinned. 'Anyway, we don't know each other too well. We just met tonight.' Then I had an idea. 'In fact, to tell you how little Mr. Dentman knows me, he's wondering whether my word is any good.'

The uneven mountain range which was his face broke out in a fresh series of divides and ridges.

'You're putting me on,' he accused. 'Your word is good any place in town. Everybody knows that.'

'You're right,' interjected Dentman. 'It was just a rib.'

Beef nodded ponderously.

'Figured it had to be,' he said gravely. 'Wait'll I tell Annie.'

He shambled away, leaving us looking at one another.

'I seem to have been told,' Dentman

admitted. Grudgingly.

'Noon tomorrow, then. Where can I reach you?'

He gave me a couple of numbers, and I scribbled them down. There was no point in prolonging the meeting. I would have liked to talk some more. Would have liked to ask, for example, whether he could bring to mind killing anybody a few hours earlier. Stuff like that. But that would all have to wait. By noon the next day the balloon would be up. We would all have a lot more on our minds than Heather Dentman's imaginary divorce.

Standing up, I nodded to my grudging host.

'Thanks for the drink. I'll call you.'

'Good.'

At the entrance, the pocket Venus flashed me a wide smile, the kind that reaches down and makes a man glow.

'You were right,' she told me. 'You're not a stranger at all. You're Mark Preston. I've heard of you.'

I smiled back, without effort.

'Just believe the good parts. The rest is slander,' I assured her. 'I heard of you, too. You're Janie. I was warned, just in time to prevent me picking you up and carting you off to a terrible fate.'

She pouted prettily.

'What stopped you?'

'Something about a black belt was mentioned.'

'Oh that.' Fingers ran lightly down my arm. 'I don't always wear it, you know.'

'Doesn't anything fall down?' I queried.

'That would depend on the company.'

We stood and looked at each other. She smelled good. I wanted to smell her a lot closer. But not tonight.

'It'll take me a couple of days to get in shape. Then I'll be back.'

She shrugged.

'If I'm still here.'

But I had a feeling she would be.

4

I tripped over Clive Barnes' body, and a hoarse voice yelled at me to quit kicking the corpses. Heather Dentman was dancing wildly on a marble plinth, while the boss-man and Chirpy-Face shouted encouragement. Beef Bronowitz came in, with little Janie sitting on his shoulder. All she had on was a black belt. In one corner, a man turned around, and he was George Dentman, with a sawn-off shotgun in his hand. He held the gun against Heather's naked middle and pulled the trigger. There was blood everywhere. Black blood, with small twinkling lights flashing from it. Far away, a bell clanged. Then again.

'Nice party, ain't it?'

Shorty leered at me obscenely. I grabbed the nearest thing I could find to smash into his stupid face. It was hard and heavy, and I couldn't lift it. I swore, and tugged, feeling sweat running down my face, into my eyes. I blinked furiously, and daylight seared at my eyeballs. Why didn't somebody stop that bell?

I was lying halfway out of bed, my right hand like a vice around the bedpost. My eyes shut again.

A dream? Cautiously, I raised the lids. Just a fraction. They'd all gone. Including Shortie, so it seemed I wouldn't be needing the bedpost.

Correction. The clanging bell had not gone. It was the door-buzzer, insistent and demanding. I rolled off the bed and padded unwillingly towards the summons. When I opened the door a man stared at me.

'Mr. Preston?'

He was young, middle twenties, but those eyes had seen things ahead of his years. I mumbled something unintelligible.

'I'm a police officer.'

'Do you have anything that says so?'

But of course he had. I'd known it the moment I saw those eyes.

'C'm on in. You want some coffee?'

He looked somewhat puzzled as he

stepped inside. I was already on my way to the percolator.

'Don't you want to know what I'm doing here?' he queried.

'Sure. Naturally,' I told him. 'But first I need my coffee.'

'People usually react differently in situations of this kind.'

He made it sound as though I was affronting his professional standing.

'Well now, as to that, officer — what's your name anyway?'

'Stratfold,' he replied, 'Detective Third Grade.'

'Sure, Officer Stratfold. As I was saying, I react a lot better when I've had my coffee. And you're not the first policeman I ever saw. Why don't you sit down? This won't take a minute.'

He seemed to give up at that, parking himself stiffly in a spot where he could keep an eye on me.

'How'd you want this?'

'Black. But I'm not sure — '

'Look, what harm are you doing?' I queried. 'I'm going to drink coffee. There's nothing in the rules of the

Department to say you can't do the same. You don't believe me, read through them again.'

'I'm here on a very serious matter,' he said, in an attempt to restore the official relationship.

'Uh huh.'

I always maintain that one yardstick by which to assess the progress of twentieth century man is the increasing speed with which he can get his java heated up. Quite soon, I was passing him a cup of the scalding liquid, and sipping thankfully at my own. He wouldn't accept a cigarette. I would.

'That's better. You didn't search me for hidden weapons, by the way.'

'No, I didn't,' he confessed. 'But experience has proved to me that those machine guns tend to reveal themselves under a man's pyjamas.'

Jokes yet. I grinned faintly.

'O.K. I'm conscious. What's with this serious matter?'

'I'm from the Homicide Bureau. I think you know Lieutenant Rourke?'

Too well, I reflected.

'We're old — er — friends,' I admitted. 'But I never saw you before. What happened to Schultzie?'

'We swapped assignments for six months. He's doing my stuff on Fraud and Morals.'

'Ah. What does John want?'

'The lieutenant' — heavy emphasis on the rank — 'wants you to come with me to headquarters.'

'Could I ask why?'

'You could ask all you want. He doesn't tell me all his reasons. Just to come and get you.'

As I got busy with the coffee my mind was chasing around, trying to detect how it was that the homicide boys had connected me to the Barnes killing so fast.

'What's the charge?' I asked innocently. He frowned.

'You know as well as as I do there isn't any charge. If so, I wouldn't be sitting here like some old ladies' tea party. Just the lieutenant would like a little co-operation. Are you coming?'

'Why not? All right-thinking citizens

should co-operate with the police. Just take me a few minutes to get ready. I imagine you're going to wait?'

'Right.'

Detective Stratfold might be new to homicide, but he wasn't new to the business of being a policeman. He followed me at every turn, while I went through the routine of getting dressed and cleaned up. As I knotted the heavy green tie, he said conversationally,

'According to Records, you have a firearms certificate.'

'The Records are correct.'

'Where's the gun?'

I went to the drawer to get it. A black .44 Police Colt appeared in his hand from nowhere.

'Nothing personal,' he assured me.

But, personal or no, his weapon remained very steady as I withdrew my own gun gently and handed it over. He had a handkerchief ready in his left hand as he took it, sniffing at the snout. Then I stuck it in a side pocket. I pointed to the Colt.

'You're a cautious man.'

He nodded.

'You're right. That's what they told us at the Academy. A cautious copper is a live copper. Two of the guys in my entry weren't paying attention. I went to both funerals.'

I could see why the Department had sent him to work with Rourke.

'Since this isn't a pinch, you won't mind if I travel in my own car? I have things to do this morning.'

'O.K.'

Twenty minutes, two near misses, and three waved fists later I was nosing around the parking area outside the Monkton City Police Department head-quarters.

Like any other progressive city, Monkton has many building projects to which it can point with pride. A good library, new schools, an especially fine building to house the gatherers of taxes. Not long before, several commendations had been awarded for the enlightened and comfortable design and layout of the splendid new penitentiary. A man who has a period of years to reflect on his

66

misdeeds should be able to do it in congenial surroundings. Forward-thinking citizens applauded the humane motivation which lay behind the project.

Naturally, all these things cost money, and money is an item very dear to the hearts of the taxpayers. Only seventy years before, they had voted a substantial sum to provide a modern building for their policemen. The sheriff and his six deputies were certainly the most pampered group of law-enforcement officers in the entire State, spacewise. Since those days, the city has multiplied itself many times, and the municipal budget many more. The law enforcement needs have moved with the times, and at the last count Monkton City boasted the seventh largest police department in the State. And they all lived together in the same noble pile as those far-off hard-riding deputies. When the building was first completed, one critical citizen thought the stables were far too lavish, and queried the need for the police to have their own blacksmith's shop. As the horses moved out, men moved in, and to this day that section of buildings is referred to as Feed and Grain.

The net result is that the department now works in conditions so overcrowded and cramped that it would head any list of slum clearance projects, but for the saving factor that the people who are suffering are on the city payroll. When zealous reformers start their periodic campaigns for cleaning up our fair city, they quite naturally exclude such non vote-catching subjects as the police department. One more Quonsett hut would be the allocation.

Stratfold stood waiting for me at the entrance to the main building. We walked in together, the duty sergeant nodding casually as we passed him.

'Do we take the elevator?' I asked innocently.

The temporary homicide officer scowled.

'If I'm going to die in the line of duty, it won't be at the hands of that lethal machine. The lieutenant figures it's worth two extra men to the department. One to intimidate the wokies, and another to terrorise the suspects.'

I grinned, and we mounted the narrow, worn stairway. The office allocation for the homicide squad is three rooms. In the smallest of them Rourke sits, sharing the isolated squalor with his number two, a great bull of a man named Randall. The legend on the door reads 'Captain of Detectives', and that means Rourke. A man should be grateful for the recognition bestowed on him by the award of a title like that. That was the view taken officially, a view which was reinforced by the fact that John Rourke had never been moved up to captain status on the payroll. He was still Lieutenant Rourke, Captain of Detectives, Acting. He'd been acting that way now for years, and it was way past time for him to be given the job. The dirt on the half-glass door was the same as I remembered from my last visit.

Stratfold knocked and went in first. The grizzled Irishman stared up from his desk at the interruption, screwing his eyes to penetrate the thick, smoke-laden atmosphere.

'Well, well, the master detective. Come in sir, come in. Have a chair. Good of you to spare a few moments from your busy schedule. Did the lady make a fuss, officer?'

'Lady?' queried my puzzled escort.

'Maybe I use too high a classification. There's usually some broad involved when we call on this terror of the underworld.'

Stratfold was not accustomed to his boss's heavy-handed banter where I was concerned.

'No,' he denied, 'there was no one else in the apartment.'

Rourke raised his fierce eyebrows, and let me have the full glare of his piercing blue eyes.

'Well, well. Day off, huh? We appreciate the co-operation, Mr. Preston. Please have a chair.'

I parked, with some reluctance, in the rickety wooden seat opposite his desk. A few hours on that unstable hard surface was enough to make most people confess to anything.

'How've you been, John?'

'How I've been is fine.' Then turning to Stratfold, 'O.K. son, you have plenty of other work. I need information from this desperado, and he won't tell me a thing while you're listening.'

Stratfold nodded uncertainly and went to the door. I winked at him as he went out.

'Seems like a good officer,' I told his chief.

He grunted.

'I'll be sure and pass your commendation on to the commissioner. He likes to have the views of prominent citizens. This won't take up too much of your time. Or mine, I hope. We're both busy men, me with the city's business, and you minding everybody else's. Let's get the desk cleared. Just tell me, in a few simple words, why you knocked off Barnes.'

Luckily for me, I was by no means unused to the Irishman's little subtleties.

'Who?'

I fished around for my Old Favorites. They were no competition for the evil little Spanish cigars which Rourke smoked, but a man has to fight with what he has.

Now he sighed, a deep, theatrical sound, which was accompanied by a

71

beseeching look at the ceiling.

'Barnes,' he repeated. 'Name of Clive. Is it all coming back?'

I fanned out twin streams of smoke and shook my head.

'Barnes. No, nothing happens. I don't remember bumping off any Barnes lately. Don't let this get around, on account of my image. The truth is, I haven't bumped off anybody at all in weeks.'

'Humph.' He opened a thin brown folder. 'I thought this was going to be easy. The killer confesses right off the hook, nice quick trial, no fuss.'

'That could still happen,' I suggested. 'All you have to do is to get the right killer.'

'Which you aint?'

'Which I ain't.'

Rourke sighed, and spread his hands on the desk.

'Pity. It all fits. The gun, the witness, the finger-prints. Maybe you forgot, huh? You had a few drinks afterwards, took a couple of pills. A little memory lapse, what do they call it, temporary amnesia. It could happen to the best of us.'

I didn't like the mention of a witness. The rest was eyewash.

'Well, I'm not infallible,' I told him. 'Tell me a little more about it. Who knows, maybe it'll all come flooding back. First off, who is this Barnes?'

'He is, or was, the tennis pro down at the Bay End Club.'

'Well, there's your answer,' I exclaimed. 'Those tennis guys make more enemies than the average mobster.'

He ignored this, and bored on.

'Last night, somebody got sore at old Clive. Sore enough to put four slugs into him. From a .38. You have a .38 they tell me.'

'Not any more. Your man Stratfold just took it down to ballistics. You ought to get a report any minute.'

'Really? It'll only be confirmation. Your car has been identified as to make, year and colour, by one of Barnes' neighbours who happened to take his dog out for a walk.'

'I must make a note to unload my Ford shares.'

'What?'

'The way you tell it, Ford sold only one car that year, in my colour. The organisation must be on the slide. If your information is correct, of course. I'll get onto Detroit when I leave here.'

'All right, wise guy, what about the prints? They're all over the place. At ten cents a smudge you'd be a rich man.'

There was no fast answer to that one. Carefully, I said,

'You know, it's beginning to work. Little stirrings of memory. I believe I did call round there about something.'

'Damn right, you did. You practically climbed all over the joint. What were you looking for?'

'That's it,' I announced triumphantly. 'You brought it all back, John. Don't know how you do it. It was the letters, of course.'

'Letters?' He didn't believe a word of it.

'Yes, yes, that's it. You see, there's this rich and beautiful woman. She's crazy for Barnes. Writes him all kinds of letters. He keeps them, tied together with a blue ribbon. Then he puts in the blackmail. The woman is frantic. He threatens to tell her husband, a prominent man in the community. There'll be scandal, disgrace. Where can she turn? Then somebody tells her about me. I will recover the letters, save her honour and the family name. I wait until the house is empty, then I search the place. But I can't find them. They must be in a strong-box somewhere. This is terrible, about him being killed. I can't rest until I find the package.'

'Horse manure,' he snapped crossly. 'I saw that movie when the talkies were first invented. Honest to God, if you don't start co-operating around here, I am going to get very nasty. Anyway, there's a charge right there.'

'Charge?'

'Burglarious entry. You just admitted to it.'

I chuckled.

'You couldn't face the disgrace,' I assured him. 'You pull in a man as a suspect in a murder case, and wind up with a charge of burglary which I'll probably lick anyway. People would think you were slipping, John.'

We looked at each other for a moment, a glower from his side of the desk, a grin lacking conviction from mine. The telephone blatted away. Muttering to himself he picked it up.

A voice crackled.

'Yeah.'

Crackle.

'Yeah.'

A lot more crackling. Then Rourke grunted what might have been an acknowledgement, and cradled the receiver.

'Ballistics,' he said portentously.

I shrugged.

'So?'

'So the slugs that killed the pride of Forest Hills did not come from your gun.'

'I already told you — '

'Ah pshaw,' he scoffed. 'You told me. Is that a fact now? Did you really? Well, I'll tell you something. People tell me all kinds of stuff. You'd be amazed. You're never going to believe this, but some of the things they tell me turn out not to be true. Can you imagine? People actually tell me lies.'

'Not this people,' I demurred.

'Not about the gun. Not this time. The rest of that tired stuff you been peddling around here is strictly from fairy tales.'

He glared at me. I stuck to the part that suited me.

'The gun is clean,' I insisted.

'No it isn't,' he contradicted. 'That's another thing. The duty man in ballistics wants to file a dirty weapon complaint against the officer who owns it.'

'I'll try to do better,' I promised. 'What happens now?'

'Now we talk some more about what you were doing in the dead man's house.'

'I can't do that, John.'

'How do you mean, can't? You mean you won't. Are you by any chance throwing the Fifth Amendment at me?'

'You know I wouldn't do that. No, this is a professional matter. I have a client, and it would be against the interests of that client for me to supply you with information. You know the rules.'

'The rules say I can get a court order which compels you to answer me.'

'So get a court order.'

We stared at one another uncompromisingly.

'There's always the burglary,' he reminded me. But his heart wasn't in it.

'There is also my one phone call. Any kid on his first day out of law school could have me out of here in one hour straight.'

'That's true,' he sighed. 'Anyway the jail is crowded. What with suspects, material witnesses, and one thing and another, a man could get rich just from the coffee concession. This time you're lucky. If I find any way to slam that gate on you, Lord help you. What is this missing item, anyway? Plans for some kind of bomb?'

'Sorry, John. You'd have to ask my client.'

He picked up a pencil.

'What was that name again?'

But I'd been around too long for that one.

'Oh no, you don't. First, the court order. Then the name of the client. You must try to remember that.'

There was a tap at the door. Stratfold poked his head inside.

'Sorry lieutenant, but you said you'd be through in fifteen minutes. It's almost twenty-five already, and there's people piling up out here.'

Rourke's face was a study of alternate mauves and whites. I chuckled malevolently.

'My, my, I'm getting to be a regular old chatter-box,' I said brightly. 'Throwing your schedule all behind that way. I must be running along, John. Any time I can be of further assistance, be sure and call me.'

At the door I held out a hand towards the startled man who'd interrupted his chief.

'Do you have my property? The thirty-eight?'

He looked across at Rourke who hissed from clenched teeth.

'Give it to him. Get him the hell out of my sight. Then get your goddam ass in here and shut that door.'

I tucked the gun away, nodded cheerfully, and left them to it. Officer

79

Stratfold was about to be enlightened as to departmental procedure in the case of an investigation of homicide.

He might even learn some new words.

5

I picked up a copy of the *Globe*, and parked myself at a quiet table in a place where they crisp up the bacon the way I like it. The way I like it is underneath a heap of scrambled eggs, and keep coming with the toast.

The Barnes murder was on page four, and restricted to a neat three columns of more or less factual information. That's the trouble with buying a reliable newspaper. With the tabloids, he'd be on the front page, along with a couple of thousand words of speculation, irrelevant gossip, and what are our police doing to protect decent people against this kind of outrage.

Barnes had been thirty-four years old, with one high-school marriage behind him which ended in divorce thirteen years earlier. The name of his ex-wife was not quoted. The tabloids wouldn't be so delicate. There was a lot of stuff about his tennis career. All it amounted to was that he was like a lot of other people. Plenty of early promise, one or two important successes, but finally not really major-league material. Good, but not good enough. A familiar enough story, and one you could hear in every clubhouse in every major sport. The sister got a mention. She was a Mrs. Polly Knight, age twenty-seven, and away from her Sacramento home on a vacation. She was probably unaware of the tragedy, etcetera. Mister Polly Knight, if there was one, was not referred to. The *Globe* hadn't dug up any scandal about Barnes, and left the reader with the general impression that he'd been a popular man, moderately successful, without large dark areas in his life. H'm.

'More coffee?'

This one was blonde with the pert attraction of any nineteen-year-old working her way through college.

'Thank you.'

'I see you're reading about the murder,' she chattered brightly. 'Isn't it terrible? He was such a nice man. I mean, you know, really nice.'

That made me give her more attention. I asked casually,

'Friend of yours?'

She grinned. If everybody had teeth like that, the toothpaste mob would have to look for new jobs.

'Well, not exactly. I took instruction from him two days a week out at Monkton High. Along with twenty others. He's been doing that for ten years. If a girl qualifies to call herself a friend under those circumtances, well then I guess Mr. Barnes had a heap of friends.'

'Hey miss, how 'bout a little service here.'

A peevish call from the counter made me look across to a frowning dark-haired boy who had swivelled around on the tall stool. The glass in front of him was half-full.

'You seem to be needed.'

She wrinkled up her pretty face in pretended disgust.

'It's only Walt. Take no notice of him. He thinks he's my boyfriend.'

'And isn't he?'

She chuckled.

'I believe in the Barnes approach. Twenty at a time.'

'Any time there's a vacancy on the course,' I offered solemnly.

That brought me a quick wink, and she went away. I looked back at the picture of the smiling man who was now dead, and wondered. If a man was really in the lover business in a serious way, Barnes certainly had the right opportunities. The cream of the crop of the senior class at Monkton High, with guaranteed fresh replacements once per year. Add to that the bored wives, the divorcees and the widows out at the tennis club, and the field was wide open. I speculated dreamily on the possibilities. At the rate of one per fortnight, a man would use up say two dozen in a full year, and still leave a month clear for vacation. Well, not so much a vacation as a rest. Yes. That would be it. A man would need the rest. And to make the whole thing viable, finance-wise, he could parcel them up every few months, and sell them off as ready-made harems to those oil-billionaires over in the Middle East.

It's amazing how the mind will travel on a steady intake of scrambled eggs and bacon. Crisp bacon.

I yanked my thoughts back to more solid and profitable work. The oil-boys would have to wait. The only woman whom I could be sure of was Heather Dentman. And, I reminded myself, there was always the possibility that I was judging Barnes too hastily. There was always a chance that he'd been telling her the truth. A chance that the blackmail really was coming from some third party. It wouldn't be long before the truth about that would emerge. Barnes was dead. If the blackmail threat was repeated, then I'd had him wrong. Added to which, I hadn't been able to put my hands on those letters. At the thought of them, I smiled inwardly. I had told Rourke nothing but the truth, but in such a way it was an insult to his intelligence. All the same, he would never be able to deny that I did tell him.

I left some bills on the table, and went

out to find a pay-phone.

At the fourth ring a voice said, 'Yes?'

A woman's voice, guarded.

'Mrs. Dentman?'

'Who is this?'

'Preston, Mark Preston. We talked yesterday.'

It didn't bring the eager response a man likes to visualise.

'Mr. Preston? Oh yes. Yes, of course. Forgive me, I was late up this morning. There's still some wool around in my head.'

Normal. No strain, no worry, no caution. It wasn't right. It just wasn't any way what it ought to be, considering the man she claimed to love was the newest customer at the morgue. The explanation seemed unlikely, but I wondered whether it was possible she didn't yet know anything about it. If that was the situation, she certainly wasn't going to hear it from me over the telephone.

'There's been a development, Mrs. Dentman. I have to see you. When would it be possible?' Then, remembering my noon commitment to her husband, I added, 'Before eleven, in any case.'

'Can't you tell me about it now?'

'I'm afraid not.'

'Well,' pause, 'in that case, could you come over around ten-thirty?'

'I don't think I should do that. Come to the apartment, I mean. At this stage, it wouldn't be in your interests or mine for anyone to connect us.'

And anyone would, I reminded myself. Anyone named Hackett, the security man, plus anyone else he chose to tell. Which would certainly include the lady's husband.

'It all seems very mysterious, but if you think it's absolutely necessary — '

She left it for me to complete.

'I'm afraid it is. And you'll think so too, when you hear about it. What we need is a nice public place. Nowhere is better for a private meeting, believe me. How about the zoo?'

'The zoo?' she echoed. 'I haven't been to the zoo since I was a small girl.'

'Then it's time you brightened up the lives of those poor, dumb creatures.

There's a new fountain. It's located close by the tropical bird cages. You probably read about it. There was quite a lot of comment.'

She laughed softly.

'If it's the one that caused all the stir last year, I'm not sure I'm sophisticated enough to see it. But ten-thirty, you say? Very well, I'll be there.'

'Thank you. And Mrs. Dentman, our business yesterday was confidential only. As of this morning, it's a secret. I mean that. I don't want you to tell anyone, including your closest friend, that you and I are connected in any way at all. Believe me, I speak in your interest.'

She thought about that, then said, in a more serious tone,

'You're beginning to worry me. Shall we say ten-fifteen?'

'Better yet. Ten-fifteen it is.'

I hung up and went to my office. Florence Digby peered at me over the top of her executive horn-rims.

'Good morning, Mr. Preston.'

'Lo, Florence. Any new business today?'

'Not so far. Of course, it's early yet.'

No one else would have known it from her tone, and certainly not from her innocent expression, but Miss Digby was telling me I was early for work. For once.

'How about calls?'

'Two. Rather puzzling, I find them. Perhaps you will be able to understand them.'

'Try me.'

She looked down at her pad.

'First, a call from a man who wouldn't give me his name. He wanted to speak to you urgently. He said you would know who he was. You were talking with him last night, close to a consignment of beef.'

She raised her head to inspect my reaction.

Beef. A second or two before it clicked. It had to be a reference to a man known one-time as the White Gorilla.

'How did he speak, this man?'

'He sounded like a gentleman.'

There she went again, with those social classifications of hers. The man would have to be George Dentman.

'And the other call?'

'From a Mr. Harris. Most strange. He said I was to tell you it was Christmas, which is odd enough by itself. Then he went on to say there were four hundred and thirty-two fish due for collection by you when you were ready. He'd already eaten his.'

So one of Mournful's surefire certainties at last found its way to the winning post. I was four hundred bucks plus ahead of the game, and that was after his commission.

'Well that's good news anyway,' I told the freshly-laundered information centre. 'I'll bet he didn't sound like any gentleman?'

'Not in a hundred years,' she sniffed. 'Mr. Harris added that he had some other good business leads, if you were interested.'

No, I decided. He'd had his winner. Christmas comes but once a year, as the saying goes. The thing to do would be to take the money, and run.

Florence Digby removed her spectacles, and looked at me very directly.

'Mr. Preston, I want to ask you

something. Forgive me if you don't like it, but I think I have a right after all this time.'

A very serious approach for that hour of the morning. It could only be a raise.

'I'd have to hear it first.'

'If you are thinking of diversifying, I think I should be told about it. After all, I am the one who is left here most of the time, dealing with callers and enquiries.'

'Diversifying?' My mouth didn't exactly drop open, but I must have looked as mystified as I felt. 'How's that?'

'These calls,' she tapped imperatively at her notes. 'You met a man, obviously a well-connected man, in some meat warehouses. Another man says your fish are awaiting collection. Meat, Mr. Preston. Fish. The coincidence is too strong to be disregarded. Are we about to move into some food product business field?'

The steady eyes held nothing but serious enquiry. It was difficult to restrain from laughing, but I didn't want to cause her offence. Keeping my tone as level as I could, I said,

'No, Miss Digby. By no means. These

references are slang, I'm afraid. Misuse of the language. Nothing more. The beef is a reference to a man, the fish means money.'

Her grave expression absorbed this without flinching.

'Ye Gods,' she exclaimed.

'And little fishes,' I supplemented. 'See what I mean?'

'Hrmph.'

I always say that a Digby sniff can be heard further away than any other sniff.

I'm going to have that measured scientifically one of these days.

6

The Monkton City Zoo and Aquarium was one of the better pieces of planning by the early authorities. They gave it eighty acres of ground, and positioned it three miles from town, which was a lot smarter move than they could have foreseen. In many other parts of the country, zoos were established right on the outskirts of town, with the inevitable result that they were quickly overtaken by creeping development as the town grew. The fresh green grass became discouraged and blackened by belching smoke from industrial chimneys, and later the oil fume deposits from a population that now moved on wheels. Animals which should be breathing the cool clean air of the high savannah, struggled to adapt their lungs to this new ozone formula. Six parts gasoline, three parts tobacco smoke, one part air.

Not so the fortunate population of our

own zoo. Bright-eyed and healthy, the animals adapt quickly to an environment not so far removed from their natural habitat. The major difference is the passing presence of a two-legged animal not often seen back home where they came from. A strange kind of neighbour, who didn't want to fight or mate, and who was in consequence something of a mystery, but harmless enough on the whole.

I arrived early for my appointment with Heather Dentman, and strolled along the well-posted system of pathways towards the site of the new fountain. This had caused a fine uproar when it was first installed, and not merely because of the quarter million dollar appropriation. One of our leading sculptors had designed and made the statues of the animals which formed the structure, from the Kong-like ape at the pinnacle downwards. The creator had studied abroad a good deal, and in consequence had some distinctly European ideas about the sources and distribution of water in relation to animals. Newspapers which supported the administration had to admit the result was 'decidedly original'. Opposition sheets settled for 'downright obscene'. It was the first time I'd taken a look at the fountain at first hand, and I had to admit it strayed somewhat from the conventional.

With five minutes still to spare, I went to take a look at an old friend in the Tropical Bird Park. A large handsome mynah-bird, who didn't seem to have changed position very much since I'd last seen him. People drifted by, checking him against the little booklet they'd bought at the gate, pointing and passing on. He'd seen it all before, and sat there impassively, only a slight movement occasionally from those bright cold eyes to indicate that he wasn't a statue.

'I thought they were supposed to be able to talk?'

A complaining voice came from a brown-haired girl, who stood there, arms wrapped around a young, scrubheaded sailor. The bird swivelled his eyes one tenth of an inch. I winked at him and waited.

'Not always,' asserted the pride of the fleet. 'They're not really that smart, you know. They have to be taught by men.'

The mynah lifted one of his enormous talons, and muttered something in Chinese. The girl squealed.

'There you are. He does talk. But some kind of foreign, wasn't it? What use is that?'

'Not much,' agreed her escort. 'That was French, I think. You'd think an American zoo would have a bird you could talk to in your own language.'

He passed an appreciative hand over the girl's rump. She squeezed his arm.

'Right,' she sighed. 'We got enough foreigners over here as it is. Dumb bird.'

The mynah replaced his foot into its firm, gripping position, and stared at them malevolently.

'Screw the broad,' he advised.

The girl gave a small squeal, and the sailor looked flustered.

'You shut your mouth,' he said nastily, glaring at the source of this new advice.

'Screw the broad. Merry Christmas. Screw the broad.'

'Art, are you just going to stand there?' demanded the girl.

The sailor rolled his eyes in despair, saw me watching. I shrugged.

'He knows a lot more than that,' I advised. 'It's no place for a lady.'

'The man is right. Let's move along, honey.'

He dragged the girl away, protesting. I looked at the bird severely.

'You oughta be ashamed,' I told him.

By way of reply, he gave me some advice. It was far more specific than his earlier utterings. I decided the new fountain was having a vulgarising effect on the surrounding creatures, and went off to find Heather Dentman.

She was standing, with her back to one of the stone lions, trying not to look like a girl who was waiting for someone. Not that she'd have had to wait long. The simple white sharkskin dress was cut to emphasise the swell and thrust in all those places where a lady is expected to swell and thrust. She looked every inch what she was. Well-groomed, poised, expensive. One or two of the passing men gave me unfriendly looks as I walked up to her.

'Right on time, Mrs. Dentman,' I greeted.

'Oh, hallo. You're being very mysterious.'

It was evident from her words and her whole attitude that she hadn't heard what had happened to the boyfriend. I took her by the elbow and steered her towards a stone bench.

'We have to talk, and I think it would be better if we sat down.'

She looked mildly puzzled, but made no demur. I didn't think it was necessary to tell her why I preferred to sit. It was because I was afraid she might pass out when I told her about Barnes. Catching a fainting woman always looks so easy on the movies. Out in the real live air, it's the very devil.

I lit an Old Favorite while I tried to get the words together.

'Something's happened, hasn't it? Something bad.'

Her tone was low, but controlled.

'Yes it has, and I would be very relieved

to be a long way from here, right this minute.'

We looked at each other, faces not two feet apart.

'It's Clive, isn't it? He's hurt. There's been an accident.'

This was all wrong. I'd been going to work my way up to it in stages. It's this intuition women have for zooming in on the target.

'I'm afraid so,' I nodded. 'You'd better brace yourself, Mrs. Dentman. Clive Barnes is dead.'

Her face drained of color.

'Dead,' she repeated dully.

'Yes.'

I was waiting to support her if she began to sway. There was no need. She sat perfectly still, face towards me, but dragged heavily on the cigarette, and kept silent. A tremor went through the sitting woman, and she clasped her hands tightly together. A large tear appeared suddenly at the corner of one eye, then the other. They rolled unheeded down her cheeks.

'How? How did it happen?'

'He was murdered. Last evening, early.

I went to the house, to talk with him. When I got inside, I found him there.'

'I see.'

She took a huge, shuddering breath, and fished in her purse. A small handkerchief appeared, and she dabbed at her face.

'Don't look so worried. I'm not going to make a scene,' she assured me. 'I've always felt that what there was between us would end in some kind of disaster. But this — '

I didn't take her assurance too seriously. I've seen people control themselves before under similar circumstances, then erupt quite suddenly some time later.

'This was last night, you say? Why did you take so long to tell me?'

A natural enough question. My words would have to be hand-picked, and with care.

'As to that, there are a number of reasons,' I began slowly. 'In the first place, it was quite a while before I was able to talk to anybody about anything. The killer was still in the house. I had no way of knowing that. The first inkling I had was when I got clunked on the back of the head. I was unconscious for hours.'

My fingers strayed automatically to the swelling.

'When I came to,' I continued, 'I was alone. My first instinct was to get out of there as fast as I could.'

'You mean you didn't call the police?'

It was not so much a question as a criticism.

'No. You mustn't forget the circumstances. Barnes was dead. There was nothing I could have done to help him. I was there because you hired me. That made you my number one concern. I had to look for those letters — no, I didn't find them — and then I had to get clear, before I was found there. The police would have asked questions. Lots of questions. The answers would have done your cause no good at all, Mrs. Dentman. In the first place, you would have been a prime suspect, and the whole business would have made the front page of every sheet in town. Not exactly what you had in mind.'

I stopped talking for a moment, to let that sink in. A little colour was coming back into her cheeks.

'Could I have one of those, please?'

She pointed to the cigarette between my fingers. I fished out the pack, and tapped one free. The tube was steady in her hand as she puffed inexpertly at the lighter flame.

'I haven't smoked in years,' she remarked pointlessly. 'You said I would be suspected, in the first place. What about the second place?'

'In the second place, even if you weren't under any serious suspicion, the question of the blackmail would have become known. Either way, you would have been in serious trouble. Now do you understand?'

'I think so. Thank you. I'm afraid it will be a little while before I'm thinking clearly. But yes, yes, I can follow your reasoning. And I'm grateful.'

She was handling herself well, so far. I hoped she'd be able to keep it up. The bad news wasn't all told yet.

'There is a possibility that whoever

102

holds your letters is the same person who killed Clive Barnes,' I said, keeping my tone impartial. 'On the whole, I incline to think the two things are not connected. The blackmailer has what he wants. Why complicate things? So I think we have to assume our friend with the letters is not the killer.'

'From the way you speak, there's a conclusion to be drawn from that,' she cut in. 'I don't yet see what it is.'

I wished I didn't have to tell her.

'The conclusion is, that the price will go up. Up until now, it was a private matter. A family matter. The value of the letters was in keeping the affair a secret from your mother-in-law. Nobody else would have been especially interested. Things are different now. It's all front-page news. It's even possible you may no longer be the prime target.'

That brought her head round sharply.

'No longer — ? I don't understand.'

'You have to look at it from his point of view. Blackmail is always a question of scale. If you weren't who you are, say, for example you were the wife of a shoe clerk.

We wouldn't be talking about twenty thousand dollars. The demand would be five hundred. Something within reach. A blackmailer has to assess his market.'

The dark head bobbed up and down.

'Yes. Yes, I see that. But if it's been decided that I can somehow raise twenty thousand — '

' — which you can,' I interjected.

'Lord knows how, but yes, somehow or other. But we're back to your shoe clerk. A change of circumstances in other directions doesn't change my circumstances. Or am I missing the point?'

'Not really. That's the kind of thinking our letter-holder will be doing. What he'll go for is a new market.'

She dragged on the cigarette, made herself cough, and dropped it disgustedly to the ground.

'Who else would be interested? The newspapers?'

'No. Your mother-in-law.'

Whatever degree of composure she had managed to regain dissolved again. Her face was again white as she asked in a shocked tone.

'Cecile? But surely not? The value of them lies in my keeping her unaware of their existence. Once she knows, the letters themselves mean nothing. It's strictly a family matter from that point on.'

I shook my head. This kind of narrow thinking was not new to me. People who are accustomed to moving in the comfortable world, where money is simply a commodity you use to buy things, can be very unworldly in some things. Strictly a family matter, forsooth. This, lady, is murder we're talking about.

'As of yesterday, that was true. As of today, we have to adjust our thinking. Your mother-in-law is a very strict lady. You told me so yourself. No scandal. If she found out about those letters, just in the family circle that is, she'd have cut off the money supply. Your own words, Mrs. Dentman.'

Then she made one of those totally irrelevant remarks that women will make sometimes.

'Since we're talking about blackmail, and now murder, and since you probably committed a crime for me by not reporting what you found, I think it's time we dropped the Mrs. Dentman, don't you? Try Heather.'

'All right, Heather. But did you take my point? If Cecile feels so strongly about these things, how would she react to the prospect of her daughter-in-law appearing prominently in a murder case? Whatever action she might decide to take against you and George, that would be a family matter, true enough. But I imagine she would go to some lengths to prevent any of it coming out. Do I read the lady wrong?'

Heather shook her head.

'No. Not a bit of it. You are absolutely right. Yes, I see it now. How much do you think he'll ask?'

She was still working on the possibility that perhaps she could raise the ante. I doubted it, but she'd had as much as she could reasonably absorb for one session.

'Who knows? We'll have to wait and see.'

'Wait and see?' she repeated tonelessly.

'Yes, I think he'll give you the first

106

crack at it. I think you'll get a call, and soon, telling you the price is up. He doesn't really want the bother of opening up a whole new lot of bargaining, if he can get what he wants from you.'

'You think he will?' she queried eagerly.

'I think there's a good chance,' I said convincingly. At least, I hoped it sounded more convincing than I felt. 'I think you should go home. Stay by the phone as much as you can today. We don't want him upset by not being able to reach you. It might make him decide not to wait. The essence here is time, Heather. All the time we can. Time to keep your mother-in-law out of this. Time for you to raise the money, if you can. And time for me to track this character down. Not that I hold out much hope of that. I have to be straight with you.'

She touched my arm hesitantly.

'I trust you. I know you'll do what you can.'

I was wondering whether I would tell her about my little meeting with her husband, and decided it was necessary.

'I wouldn't discuss this with George,' I

advised. 'Not before it's absolutely necessary.'

'But there is no possibility of my raising the money without him,' she protested.

'I've seen your husband. Last night.'

I told her about our conversation at Annie Domino's place. She listened attentively, eyes widening.

'He really thinks that? That I'm looking for evidence against him? Why would he think that, suddenly?'

'I wouldn't know. I imagine it's because he knows what business I'm in, and he couldn't think of any other reason why you would need somebody like me.'

'Perhaps. Yes, that must be it. But even so, I mean, how did he even know we'd spoken?'

'Your manager. Guy named Hackett. Old George evidently has some arrangement with the man.'

'Mr. Hackett? Spying on me?'

'They don't call it that any more. They call it safeguarding the tenants and the owners.'

'How despicable.'

'Just don't let Hackett know you're on to him,' I cautioned. 'Act as though nothing has happened.'

'I'll try,' she promised. 'What will you tell George?'

'Damned if I know,' I admitted. 'Things have crowded up on me this morning. Anyway, you can leave him to me. And now I think you should be getting back. The minute that call comes, telephone my office. Miss Digby will find me. And Heather?'

She stood up, and looked at me expectantly.

' — I'm sorry about what's happened. I know you can't share it with anybody else. I feel like some kind of relative.'

She nodded, fresh tears not far away.

'Thank you. You've been good to me over this. I know you'll do your best for me. Can I give you a lift?'

'No thanks. I have a car outside.'

She tossed back her head, in a gesture almost of defiance, and walked away. I wondered how a woman like that could get herself in this kind of jam.

But then, I reflected, if there weren't

women like that there wouldn't be so many jams.

On the way out, I made a detour past the mynah-bird. He was still relishing his victory over the sailor.

'You're disgusting,' I told him.

He stared at me with deep contempt.

'Dames are dumb,' he announced. 'Dames are dumb.'

Well, it's a point of view.

7

The Motor Vehicle Bureau occupies the street level floor of one of our shiny new office blocks. I stood at the enquiries counter and pinged the bell. The police officer who came to investigate the disturbance was a medium-height square woman. Iron gray hair, cropped short, no make-up, an aggressive look behind the thick, tortoise-shell glasses.

'Oh, it's you.'

'Nice to see you too, Baxie,' I assured her.

'Sergeant Bax to you. Baxie is for my friends,' she snapped.

'But we're old buddies,' I protested.

'Huh,' she snorted. 'You come in here, maybe once a year, grab all the information you can get, and breeze out again. Not exactly a life-long friendship, I wouldn't say.'

I leaned on the counter, and pleaded with her.

'You know I'd be here every day, if there was any hope,' I said brokenly. 'But a man has to learn when he's licked. You would never do anything to betray Timothy Bax, enemy of crime. How is old Tim, anyhow?'

'You're a terrible man, Preston. I used to hope you'd improve when you got older.'

'As to that,' I replied huffily, 'we'll just have to wait and see, won't we? And you didn't answer me, about Tim. How's that shoulder?'

He'd been caught in a collapsing building one time, going back once too often to rescue the elderly inmates. The shoulder had never really mended.

'Some days are better than others. He has to avoid draughts as much as he can. Easier said than done. Until a thing like that happens, nobody realises just how much time they spend in draughty situations.'

'I imagine so. Well give him my regards, won't you?'

'If he can remember who you are.' But there was no bite behind the words. Hilda

Bax was a one-man woman, and that man was husband Timothy. Anyone who wanted to know about his shoulder couldn't be all bad. 'Now, come on. You didn't come here to talk about Tim.'

'You're right. I almost forgot.' I put an enquiry form in front of me, scribbling at the entries. 'An insurance thing. And I probably have the wrong car anyway. But at least it's a California plate.'

She picked up the form and scrutinised it.

'Wrong car, indeed,' she scoffed. 'It's more likely the last piece in some criminal jig-saw. You'll probably get a reward of half-a-million.'

'I'll be lucky to wind up with a fifty dollar trace-fee,' I assured her.

'I'll take a look.'

She went away, to do those mysterious things people in the Bureau do. With a California plate, I knew she'd be gone no time at all. I'd smoked only half a cigarette before she was back.

'I'm assuming you still have an up-to-date licence,' she quizzed.

'You assume correctly, officer.'

'H'mph.' She sounded sceptical, but it was all part of her act. If she'd been in any doubt, I'd have had to produce the buzzer. 'Well, this car is one of a fleet, registered to the Rent-an-Auto people. I've written down the address.'

'Thank you, officer. I'll split the half-million with you.'

She stared at me, unblinking.

'I'll settle for half the fifty bucks.'

'Ah, wouldn't we all? With half a million, a man can be generous. With fifty, he has to pay the rent. Thanks, Baxie, and take care.'

There was a drugstore close by. I took a cup of what the man claimed to be coffee and balanced it precariously on a shelf, next to a pay-phone.

'Rent-an-Auto,' sounded a bored voice. 'Can I help you?'

'Police Department,' I announced crisply. 'Motor Vehicle Bureau. Checking on one of your rentals. Who do I speak with?'

Boredom flew out the window.

'Just a minute, officer. I'll get the manager.'

Within seconds, a new voice at the other end. High-pitched, anxious.

'This is Mr. Backhouse, the manager. Can I help you, officer?'

'Take a note of this number, Mr. Backhouse. We'd like to know who would have been driving this car yesterday. In the evening, that is.'

'Certainly. Won't take a minute. Our records are our pride.'

I hung on, reflecting on that. Everybody has to have something to be proud of, I decided.

'Yes, I have it right here. Can you take the information?'

'Go ahead.'

'This Cadillac is on a one-week to a Mr. E. Levers. That's L-E-V-E-R-S. The address is Bungalow Seven, Beach Bungalow Park.'

'Got it,' I confirmed. 'One week, you say. How many days are left?'

'Three. The car is due back here, day after tomorrow. The client paid cash in advance, the full amount. I hope this doesn't mean any trouble for the company, officer?'

From his flustered tone, I judged that an affirmative answer would cause immediate collapse.

'Just routine,' I assured him. 'Probably nothing at all. Oh, one more thing. The man who hired the car, Mr. Levers, he will have had to produce his driver's licence. Do you make a note of those things?'

He didn't quite dare to be offended, but it was a close call.

'It's automatic,' he assured me. 'The hirer produced an Illinois licence.'

'Well, thank you, Mr. Backhouse, for the co-operation. We may have to send somebody along there later to inspect the record. I don't think myself it will be necessary.'

'No trouble,' he said emphatically. 'Believe me, our records are open for inspection by the police at any hour of the day.'

'Just fine, Mr. Backhouse. Goodbye.'

I stood by the phone, looking at my watch, and remembering I'd promised to contact George Dentman before noon. Only twenty minutes remained. I wouldn't be able to get out to the bungalow park, and do whatever had to be done in that time.

Fishing in my pocket, I came out with the number Dentman had given me, and put more change ready by the phone. Nobody at the other end seemed interested in the brr-brr I was listening to. Strange. Dentman had been so positive the night before. There was always a chance I had a wrong connection. To be certain, I dialled the number again. Still no reply. I scooped up the loose coins and shoved them in a pocket. It was no skin off my nose, I reflected. I had promised to call the man, and I'd kept my end. For the moment, anyway, I could put George Dentman out of my mind.

* * *

There's a good healthy sound to the title, Beach Bungalow Park. Beach has to mean sand and sea, Park conjures up a vision of grass and trees. A man would be forgiven for expecting to find a cluster of neat bungalows in a grassy meadow, just a stone's throw away from the fun-happy shoreline. That man would find his first view of the reality something of a disappointment. The place is a cluster all right. Or maybe clutter would be a better word. A sprinkling of wooden shacks, nearly bare of paint, flung down haphazardly on a patch of scrub-land, which turned into a sea of mud at the first sign of rain. Thin strips of concrete formed tenuous links between the shacks, and the man who allowed his car wheels to stray from these would spend a sweaty hour getting the tyres free of that cloying glue. The place is run on the general lines of a motel, but would never claim the title. To do that might attract the attention of the Tourist Office, with consequent inspection of such little details as sanitation and so forth, amenities which did not rate a high priority with the owners. It lay on one of the last sections of level ground, before the rising cliffs took over, leading up and away from such scenes, and more in the direction of developments like Bay Heights, where Heather Dentman lived. People like her probably never suspected there was such a place as the Beach Bungalow Park. People like me get paid to know things like that.

I rounded the last sweeping bend which would lead past the entrance to this blot on the landscape, and was mildly surprised to note signs of some activity at the place. As I got closer I could make out more detail. Half a dozen automobiles were parked around the front gate, something I'd never expected to see. As I got closer, a firetruck suddenly appeared, swinging out of the gate, and heading back towards town. There was no siren, so it wasn't aiming for a fire. That could only mean one thing. It left one.

Parking as close as I could get to the broken wooden fencing that made a show of enclosing the approach, I climbed out, walking past the little group of cars. Two of them had 'Press' stickers on the windscreen. Another one said 'Police'. The first shack inside had a wooden board with the hand-painted announcement, Office. A little knot of men stood around outside, smoking and talking. I saw a couple of faces I knew, and spoke to a man from the *Record*.

'Hi, Cliff. What's all the excitement?'

Gyp Clifford turned to see who it was.

'Preston. What brings you here?'

At the mention of the name, some of the others stopped chattering to take a look at me.

'Only the sight of you guys. I'm just on my way to pay a call up on the cliffs. What brings the gentlemen of the Press?'

'Fire,' he told me, in a bored voice. 'Some nut put a match to one of these choice developments.'

But I knew there had to be more.

'Come on Gyp, what's all the mystery? The Record doesn't send a man with his own by-line, just because some crank burnt a heap of wood. It's work for a kid from college.'

'Well,' he admitted grudgingly, 'it is a little more complicated. The guy with the torch forgot to empty the building first.'

'There were people inside?'

'You got it. Two men. We're waiting to talk to the manager man, soon as the cops get through with him.'

An unwelcome thought was beginning

to form in my mind, but I didn't dare ask too many questions. With people like Clifford, and these other bored-looking characters, one wrong word can turn them into a pack of baying hounds.

'Too bad,' I said indifferently. Then, as though a sudden thought occurred, I added quietly, 'say, did the insurance boys get this covered yet?'

'Haven't seen any. Why?'

'You know how it is. Case like this, Johnny-on-the-Spot might notice something useful from the insurance angle. Since I took the trouble to pull up, I might as well see if I can spot anything. Always assuming the joint carries any insurance in the first place. Think I'll take a look.'

'Suit yourself. There's nothing to see you couldn't find after any firework party.'

I looked innocently into the distance.

'Which one was it?'

He raised an uninterested arm.

'Out there on the left. They claim it's number seven. As though any man could tell one of these joints from another.'

Clifford had evidently decided he'd spent quite enough this warm day on a fairly unexciting story.

'Well thanks.'

I nodded and strolled away. The others lost interest in me at once. Just another rubberneck.

Anywhere else, the surrounding properties would have produced anxious, worried neighbours. People who were all excited with the comings and goings. Policemen, firemen, newspaper reporters. These are the very stuff of the headline news, and it's only natural that anyone in the vicinity is going to stand and goggle. In most vicinities, that is. In this secluded development — 'Away from the Bustle of the City' — people weren't interested in what happened to other people. Not even in policemen, firemen and newshawks. Especially policemen.

There was no sign of life from any of the surrounding bungalows as I walked towards the scene of fire. But I could feel hidden eyes on me as I passed by. Was I going to be the one who knocked on the door and began asking questions?

Questions that might quickly become difficult to answer? And were nothing to do with what had happened at number seven? I passed a screen of straggly hopeless bushes, and got my first sight of the damage. Gyp Clifford had been right. It looked less like a fire-damaged residence than a kid's bonfire. There was a lingering smell in the air, that recognition recoiled from. Thin smoke still rose lazily, from charred heaps of wood, as a kneeling man rose at my approach, dusting off his hands.

'Well well, the poor man's Sherlock Holmes.'

He was Lyle Merkoff, an investigator from the fire marshall's office, and we knew each other. People claimed Merkoff could look at a burnt hotel towel, and order the apprehension of a forty-seven year old Chinaman with two gold teeth. Even allowing for some degree of exaggeration in that claim, there was no disputing that he was a very smart copper in any league.

'Hi, Lyle, what's coming off?'

He frowned, and screwed up his eyes.

'Well now, as to that, I was about to ask you the same thing. Here we have a nice quiet arson, with double murder on a side dish, and who turns up to the feast but you. Or maybe you just stopped by for a pack of cigarettes on this busy street?'

The trouble with police work, it distorts a man's mind. Nothing is ever straightforward. I told him the same tale I'd given Clifford. It seemed to satisfy him.

'You're wasting your time,' he assured me. 'This whole thing is cut and dried.'

'But you did say arson,' I objected mildly. 'And murder. How do you know it wasn't a simple accident?'

It was precisely the kind of damnfool elementary question that stings the pride of a professional. And it usually produces precisely the kind of reply I got. And wanted.

'How do I know?' he said nastily. 'Because I spent fifteen years of my life learning my business, that's how I know. Because an accident happens in one place and spreads. It doesn't happen in four different places within seconds. That's how I know. And it doesn't prevent two grown men from opening a simple door. Not the way this does. That's how I know.'

'This' was a half-hoop of metal, with a charred rope attached.

'What is that? Remains of some kind of bomb?'

He threw up his hands in despair, and looked upwards for some help in dealing with this moron.

'Bomb?' he echoed. 'Does it look like a bomb? Why does everything have to be so dramatic for the public? It's what it looks like, Preston. It's a door-handle. From the outside of the door. And this,' he jabbed a stubby forefinger at the piece of rope, 'this complicated piece of bomb mechanism is called rope. What you do, if you have somebody inside, and you want to prevent them getting outside, you tie a piece of this complicated rope to the door-handle, and you fix the other end to something else. In this case a simple stake in the ground. That stake there, to your right.'

I shuddered. And I meant it.

'It's that simple? And two men are dead?'

'Right. And so it's murder. Two murders.'

I was bothered about the number. I'd been hoping to find three men when I came out in the first place. Alive.

'Who were they, Lyle? Local people?'

'Business guys, I heard. From out of town. I don't know what business they were supposed to be in. Whatever it was, they both carried guns. Not exactly brush salesmen, I wouldn't have said.'

I would have liked to ask a lot more questions, but to do that would not have fitted with the story I'd told him. In particular I wanted to know which of the three men I'd talked with at Clive Barnes' house was still alive.

'Well, nice talking with you, Lyle. There's nothing here for me. But it's always worth taking a look.'

'Ghoul. I'll see you.'

He had a pair of tweezers in his hand, as he knelt again and began sifting delicately at the ruins. I walked away briskly, glad to be away from the

126

questions and the scene. Glad to leave behind that sweet smell of burning which didn't originate from wood.

As I got back in the car I realised something I'd forgotten in the new excitement. The Cadillac, the one rented by Mr. Levers from Rent-an-Auto, was nowhere in sight. It was reasonable to assume that whichever of the three survived the fire, would be wherever the car was.

And I was probably the only man in town who knew what he looked like.

8

Seeing that I was already out in the right direction, I decided it would do no harm to pay a call at the Bay End Club. As distance goes, it was about five miles and ten million dollars east of the Beach Bungalow Park.

Here were lush lawns, with swivelling sprinklers playing quietly over the grass. There wasn't so much a clubhouse as a club complex, with a separate restaurant and bar, members' lounge and reading room forming the main structure. To the left, locker rooms for the tennis members, with the professional's own room standing apart. To the right, similar accommodation for the golf members. Joining the club was a simple matter. All you were required to produce was a bank-roll of a couple of million dollars, and a family with a few judges and senators in the background. The rules were even elastic as to these last qualifications. If you could show five million, nobody looked too hard for the political pull. Although, when you come to think of it, it wasn't much of a concession at that. Without that kind of influence, how does anyone lay hands on that kind of money?

I left the car where it wouldn't give offence to the gleaming limousines lined up outside, and walked into the main entrance. There wasn't any guard, but that was no surprise. There would be nothing in the place worth stealing. These were not cash people. Smiles, handshakes and signatures. These were their currency, and it was to be doubted whether any one man carried more than twenty or thirty dollars.

The interior was cool, and furnished elegantly in the Spanish style. Not the Spanish of the chile joints, but the hacienda Spanish of Old Spain. It wasn't the kind of place for signposts, and I was wondering which way to go when a door opened down a passage to my left, and I heard voices. One of them was angry.

'Don't think you can get away with

this, Freddie. You haven't seen the last of me.'

A second voice, quiet but firm.

'I'm extremely sorry you should take this as a personal issue. I'm only passing on to you the decision of the committee.'

'Yeah, well, we'll see about your damn committee.'

A man stomped towards me, red-faced and cursing furiously to himself. I stood to one side to let him pass. He glared at me, as though trying to decide whether I was a member of this damn committee, decided not and swept past.

I went down to the door he'd left open, and peeked inside. The man with the quiet voice was just resettling himself behind an aged leather-top desk. He looked up enquiringly.

'Good afternoon,' he said pleasantly. 'Can I help you?'

'I'm looking for the club secretary,' I told him.

'You have the right man. My name is Arbuthnott. What can I do for you?'

He was fifty years old, with a good-humoured face that had seen plenty of sun. Even the top of the near-bald head was weatherbeaten. Despite the heat of the outside day, he wore a correct collar and tie along with the business suit. Unable to mind my own business, as always, I ventured,

'I'm glad to find you O.K., Mr. Arbuthnott. Some man pushed past me just now as though he'd been in a fight.'

He smiled faintly.

'You wouldn't believe it, but there are still people who think all they have to do to join the club is spread a few dollars around and keep pushing. As to a fight, well, not many of them want to take it quite that far.'

He pointed to a framed photograph on the wall. It showed a younger Freddie, in ring clothes. I walked over to read the caption, which announced that he'd been the State Universities' welter-weight champion back in the fifties.

'I'm glad I didn't come to fight.'

This brought me a light chuckle.

'With a name like Arbuthnott, you either fight or the wolves get you. Now, just why did you come, Mr. — ?'

'Preston.'

I went over to the desk and showed him my identification.

'Oh dear, I hope we're not going to have any scandal.'

'Nothing like that,' I assured him. 'I'm here because of what happened to Clive Barnes.'

A frown creased into the suntan.

'That's a bad business,' he said slowly. 'The police came out this morning. There wasn't anything much I could tell them about him. He was a good player, good coach, popular with the members. He didn't get noisy in the bar, and he didn't get too personal with the ladies. Or rather, if he did, none of them ever complained about it.'

He raised his eyebrows to see if I knew what he meant. I knew what he meant. The tennis professional is natural prey for any man-eater with too much money, and time on her hands. It wasn't to be expected that they would overlook a prospect like Barnes. Freddie was saying that Barnes knew how to deal with things.

I smiled.

'Matter of fact, that brings me right to the point. One of your members asked me to come out here. A Mrs. Heather Dentman?'

'Mrs. Dentman, yes.' There was a tinge of anxiety behind the words. 'A charming woman. Charming. Useful player, too. Did quite well in our singles competition last year. Got to the fourth round, if I remember rightly. What can I do for her?'

'She was at the club quite recently. She hadn't intended to play that day, but somehow she was needed to make up a four. She was wearing a watch, very expensive, not the kind of thing she would want to leave in a locker, and ordinarily she would have left it at home. But when she accepted a game, she wanted someone to look after it. The obvious person was Barnes. He had a room of his own, and it would be quite safe. After the game, she forgot all about it, and went off home. Later, when she remembered, she wasn't at all concerned. The watch would be quite safe with Barnes until the next time she came out here. But then today, after she heard what

133

happened, she realised other people would be going into his room. Perhaps the wise thing to do would be to ask me to come out and get it back. You know how things can get mislaid once someone dies.'

He wasn't too receptive.

'Of course, Mrs. Dentman knows her own business best,' he demurred, 'but it seems like a lot of trouble. To employ an expensive man like you, when all she had to do was pick up a telephone.'

But I'd expected that.

'You're quite right, but that isn't the way it was. I'm already working for the family on something quite different. I just happened to mention I'd be coming out in this direction, and she asked if I'd make a detour and pick up the watch at the same time.'

'I see. It's very valuable, you say?'

'About twelve hundred dollars, she told me. I think it's ridiculous, frankly. A woman can be just as late for her appointment with a sixteen fifty Club Timer.'

That brought a better reaction.

'It's the diamonds,' he explained. 'Cooler on the wrist in this hot weather. Well, let's go and take a look.'

I didn't really want him along. If those letters were in the late pro's room, I couldn't mistake them for a watch. But I grinned as though he had a great idea, and we walked out together. In the locker-room, a short dark man wagged his head.

'Afternoon, Mr. Arbuthnott.'

'Hallo George. Shouldn't you be on court maintenance today?'

'Yes, I should. This is putting me all behind. But Charlie called in sick, and the members would put up a squawk if there wasn't nobody in here looking after their stuff.'

Freddie nodded impatiently.

'What's wrong with Charlie?'

'Head cold, I think. A couple of days he said.'

'Well, we'll just have to make do.'

He led me past the rows of lockers and out the far end. Producing a bunch of keys he opened a door, and said,

'This is the tennis pro's room.'

It wasn't much. One table, a chair, a day couch, and two cupboards jammed with equipment. Freddie waved a hand around.

'Help yourself. A watch could be anywhere.'

Ten minutes later, there was no hole in that room I hadn't dug into. No letters. I said cheerfully,

'I guess what happened was, the day Mrs. Dentman left the watch with him, Barnes found she'd gone off without it. He decided it wouldn't be safe, leaving a thing like that here overnight. He probably took it home with him. That's where we'll find it.'

Freddie nodded.

'I hope you're right. Not the kind of thing I like. A valuable watch going astray like that. Not good for the club.'

'Oh, I shouldn't make too much of it,' I said consolingly. 'Mrs. Dentman only blames herself for being careless. It'll turn up.'

'I hope you're right,' he repeated. 'We have a big responsibility here. Our members like to feel they can treat this place like their own homes. Everybody on my staff is trusted like a member of the family.'

'Of course they are,' I soothed, 'and it's justified. The reputation of this club is known way outside the city. I've heard it referred to in many places. One little watch is not going to change that. And there's nothing to say it's even lost.'

'You'll let me know if you find it? Whatever you say, I shall most certainly worry.'

'You can count on it. Believe me, you're far more concerned than the lady who owns it.'

'You're probably right. Well, I'd better get back to my office. The morning crowd will be coming back any moment. One of my jobs is listening to how they missed a sitter at the twelfth. If there's nothing else — ?'

'You've been very helpful. Thanks again. I'll go out this way.'

We shook hands, and he went off to listen to his daily quota of bad-luck yarns from the returning golfers. I went back to where the disconsolate George stood, staring out at the dull red tennis courts. He looked round at my approach.

'It's that base-line on number three worries me,' he grumbled. 'All chewed up. People argue about whether a ball is in or out. Wouldn't take me an hour. They'll complain, you know.'

'Well, it isn't your fault. You have to stand in when Charlie doesn't turn up.'

'Head-cold,' he sniffed. 'I wouldn't stay home with no head-cold.'

'Some of us have a stronger sense of duty than others. Tell you what I'll do. I'm going back into town now. If you like, I'll call in on old Charlie. Tell him what the position is out here. Maybe he doesn't realise the jam you're in. Might even be able to persuade him to come to work. Worth a try.'

'Would you do that? Would you really? Say, I'd certainly appreciate it. Some of these members can get awful hard on a man.'

I made a note of Charlie's address, and went away, leaving George to face the demon members.

The car had taken advantage of my

absence by turning itself into a fair impression of an oven. I opened everything that would open but the temperature remained that of the average sweat-box. By the time I reached town, my thoughts were concentrated on one thing only. The thought of the shower in my apartment, and the cool fresh linen I had stashed away.

I rolled thankfully into Parkside. It was now mid-afternoon, and Frank, the day-man, looked at me in some surprise.

'Hi, Mr. Preston. Hot ain't it?'

I admitted it was hot, and walked past him.

'Been a man here from the police,' he called. 'Asked me if I knew where he could find you. I told him I didn't, unless you was down to your office.'

'Police? What did he want?'

'He wouldn't say. Just routine, he told me. He said if I saw you, I was to tell you Mr. Rourke would appreciate a call. Did I get the name right? Rourke, was that it?'

Oh yes, that was it all right. I wondered what the Irishman was up to now.

'Thanks, Frank. I expect it's about the car.'

'Sure.'

I went upstairs and climbed under the shower. Twenty minutes later, I was all fresh again. The temptation to stay around the apartment for an hour or two was strong, but time wasn't standing still, and there were an awful lot of things to do. I went regretfully back to the car and headed for the office.

9

There were voices inside as I opened the door. Florence Digby was almost indignant as she said,

'Mr. Randall, if I had any idea where Mr. Preston was, I would most certainly tell him you want to see him. Oh.'

At the sight of me, she stopped. Gil Randall stood in front of her desk. They both looked as if they had been interrupted in an argument.

'Mr. Preston, will you please explain to the sergeant that I do not have a minute by minute plan of your movements.'

'That's right, Gil, she doesn't. If it comes to that, I don't often have one myself. What's all the fuss?'

'Let's go in your office,' he growled.

I motioned him to lead the way, shooting an enquiring glance at Florence. She heaved her shoulders around in dumb show, to indicate she had no idea what he wanted.

Randall settled his enormous bulk into a chair I keep for visitors. Mostly, it looks adequate enough. With Randall spread all over it, the chair looked as if it escaped from a doll's house. The sergeant is Rourke's number two over at Homicide, a vast shambling hulk of a man, who looks as if he may be going to fall asleep any minute. You could tell just by looking at him that he would be slow in his thinking, ponderous in movement. The original dumb flatfoot come to life. You only had to see those heavy-lidded eyes to know what an effort the thought process would present to their proud owner. If you'd broken a few laws, you wouldn't be too concerned about outsmarting this Sergeant Randall. And you would still be puzzled as to what it was that went wrong when you heard that heavy key turn in the lock. Not that you could blame yourself too much. You'd meet plenty of other guys in the exercise-yard, all wondering the same thing.

I'd known him long enough not to make the mistake of under-rating him.

'What's it all about, Gil?'

'Nothing much,' he said easily. 'It's too hot for work, wouldn't you say? A man doesn't feel like rushing around.'

'That's true.'

I had an idea that anything I said was liable to be the wrong thing.

'Besides, you know, we're kind of undermanned, right now, over at the department. Everybody doing two men's work.'

'Is that a fact?'

'Yes, it is. Sometimes it works out, you know? Sometimes, a man gets two jobs, there's no connection. He goes off in all directions, wondering why he didn't take that easy number in City Hall, and then suddenly, the directions join up. Instead of two directions, three directions, suddenly it's all one direction. When that happens, believe me, this police work gets easier.'

I tapped out an Old Favorite, nodding pleasantly. All this talk about directions was not settling to the stomach. The one direction Randall was pointing had led him to my office. And it was no kind of weather for social calls.

'They work you people too hard.'

'That's right,' he grumbled. 'Believe me, it's a pleasure talking to a citizen who understands our problems. Somebody who is always willing to help when he can. Somebody like you.'

The good citizen clicked a lighter into flame, and dragged strong harmful smoke down inside him.

'Always glad to help the department,' I assured him.

He beamed.

'My exact words,' he confirmed, 'The lieutenant seemed to think you weren't being very co-operative. But I spoke up for you. I told him he was wrong. I said, Lieutenant, I said, you can believe me, Preston is not a man who will sit on his can if he thinks he can help us out with these four murders.'

Four. I almost choked on the smoke. Hoping my voice sounded more under control than my jumping thoughts, I said,

'Murders? Four murders?'

'Four,' he repeated flatly. 'Ain't it awful the way these things build up? Take this Barnes thing, for instance. I mean, you didn't seem to be too involved in that one. Not from the yarn you spun the lieutenant. A simple matter of burglary. Well, I mean to say, if we're going to start accusing every burglar in town of homicide, people will think we're slipping, right?'

As questions go, that one would be filed in the category headed 'Have you stopped beating your wife?'

'Nobody has charged me with burglary,' I returned.

'My words, exactly,' he assured me. 'A coincidence, that's what it was. What's this country coming to, if a man can't break into another man's house without everybody shouting 'burglar'. And, as to the rest of it, just because the other man gets himself bumped off, is that any reason to suspect homicide? No. That would be confused thinking. I told the lieutenant the same thing.'

The great head nodded with satisfaction. I was beginning to understand how the fly feels as he watches the spider uncurling himself from sleep, and squinting across the web.

'What's this all about, Gil?'

'Ah,' he sighed. 'What indeed? Who knows? Coincidence, is my guess. I personally think it's just coincidence. I mean, you take this morning now. You call in to have a nice chat with the lieutenant, just like any other citizen starts his day. You dicker around with little items of gossip. Burglary, homicide, that kind of stuff. Like everybody does. The coincidence comes in when you get in your car and drive off somewhere else, and guess what? The very place you go, two other guys have just been scragged. Coincidence, I say. But you know the lieutenant. He always has to suspect everybody of base motives. I wonder he can sleep nights. Personally, I think he's making a lot of fuss, just because you get mixed up in three homicides in twenty four hours. Do you have any base motives, Preston?'

'Certainly not,' I denied.

'But you didn't say you weren't there,' he pointed out. 'You didn't say old Lyle Merkoff mixed you up with somebody else.'

'I explained that to him. I happened to

be on my way for an appointment somewhere else. When I saw the crowd, the pressboys, at the bungalow park, I just stuck my nose in to find out what was going on. Anybody would have been curious.'

'We're not talking about anybody. We're talking about you. The way you keep happening all over the place.'

'Coincidence.'

He moved his head laboriously from side to side.

'I might have gone for that, if it hadn't been for this Earl Gannon connection.'

'Hows'at? Earl Who?'

'Gannon,' he supplied. 'Is it all coming back?'

'It's never been anywhere,' I assured him. 'I don't have the slightest idea what you're talking about. What's with this Gannon?'

Sleepy eyes gazed at me for long seconds.

'You don't know?'

'Right. I don't know. Who is Gannon, and where does he come in?'

'I don't think it would be right to say

he comes in, exactly. He's been in from the start. What you might call a founder-member. Tell you what I'll do. It's too hot to play games. I could put you in the slammer for a coupla days, give you a chance to think. But you perform a kind of public service while you're out and about. You keep finding work for morgue attendants and gravediggers. I'll make a deal with you. Tell me what you know, and I'll tell you what I know. A trade. Whaddya say?'

'I say I don't have any goods. It wouldn't be fair to you.'

This brought a frown.

'I'll decide what's fair. I'll even go first. It'll help you see how much trouble you could be in, if I get nasty.'

He was using words I didn't like. Words like 'slammer', 'trouble', 'nasty'. They don't make good listening coming from a man like Randall.

'It's up to you,' I shrugged.

'You bet it is. This starts with the man Gannon, like I just said. He's from the East. Turned up here in town four days ago. We didn't get tipped off because the police back there didn't miss him right off.'

'Tipped off?'

'Yeah. Gannon was in the rackets. Not big, not a top echelon man, but important enough for the law to keep an eye on him. Why he came to Monkton City we still don't know. But somebody does. And whoever that somebody is, put three slugs in him and left him on a waste lot just outside the limits.'

'Sounds like mob people.'

'Doesn't it, though? As soon as we ran his stuff through Washington, out came all this lovely background information, and we had a make. The State of Illinois were very interested to know what happened to their wandering citizen.'

I was hearing again the voice of the manager of Rent-an-Auto. He'd said the man who rented the Cadillac was a Mr. Levers. And Mr. Levers produced an Illinois driver's licence.

'This seems to be making you think,' observed Randall.

'Not really. Just paying close attention.'

'H'mph,' he grunted. 'Then we get a

buzz. Three of Mr. Gannon's business associates are missing, and could be headed our way. This is a big city we have here. We start to watch out for these tourists. Today we found two. Manny Levers and Shortie Jack Becker. They were inside that shack you looked at today. Small world, ain't it?'

So the man missing was the one who kept grinning. The one who'd turned me loose.

'You said there were three when they started out. You think the other man started the fire?'

A deep sigh came from across the room.

'No I don't. I think he got lucky. I think whoever set fire to that shack was assuming they were all inside. Wasn't you, was it?'

I was affronted.

'Now see here — '

'All right, all right.' He waved me down. 'I didn't think it was.'

He didn't offer any more. We sat there in silence for several seconds. Then I said,

'Well? Is that it?'

'That's it.'

'But I still don't follow,' I objected. 'This Gannon takes a trip out here and gets himself killed. Two of the men who follow him get the same treatment. It doesn't sound like any routine homicide to me. It sounds like racket people. I don't see what any of those people have to do with me, just because I get nosey around fires.'

He looked surprised.

'Because of Barnes. Old Clive Barnes. Didn't I tell you? According to ballistics, the gun that killed him was the same one killed Gannon. And Barnes was in no rackets, not that we know of. He had no connection with anything of that nature. A straight citizen. So the only link we can turn up, if we leave out the gun, is you. You're all we have, Preston. Now it's your turn to trade.'

There wasn't any point in further protest. No more hedging, stalling, and general word-shuffling. Randall was right. I was a prime connection with the other links in this particular chain, and the other links were all dead. Except

Chirpy-Face, who'd missed the execution. And there was no way of locating him. That left me.

'You've told me a whole lot of stuff there,' I began. 'I wasn't kidding when I said I had nothing to trade.'

He tut-tutted.

'You wanta make your one phone-call from here, or down at headquarters?'

'I already told Rourke why I went to Barnes' house.'

'The lieutenant is very bad on details. He forgets things. Why don't you try it over with me?'

Trying to make it sound less like some nineteenth century romance, I told him about the missing letters, the blackmail threat, and how it was my interpretation that Barnes cooked up the whole thing himself. Randall kept his face expressionless.

'And that's the way you got into this?'

'That's it.'

A vast expulsion of air showed his exasperation.

'Tell you what's bothering me, Preston. You've been around quite a while. You

152

have told the department some very fancy tales over the years. Real lulus. It isn't like you to come up with something so unimaginative.'

'Imagination is not involved,' I persisted. 'The reason it sounds so terrible is because it's the plain truth.'

'Maybe.'

He scratched prodigiously at his chin.

'So what do we make of it now?' he continued.

'This desperate gang of inter-state adventurers get to know about these letters. They kill Barnes to get their hands on them. They quarrel among themselves, start knocking each other off. Level with me. Does that make any kind of sense to you?'

'No, it doesn't,' I admitted.

'No, it doesn't. These are simple people we're dealing with. Protection rackets, armed robbery, horse-race fixing, stuff like that. They understand things like that. Direct action, a quick profit, a little incidental violence. That's where they live. This letter business is too subtle. Half of them can't read, outside of a sport headline. But, even so, the connection has to be there, and the only one who can put a finger on it is you. Are you going to tell me any more, or shall we be on our way?'

I had a duty to Heather Dentman. She was meeting the tab, and that made her entitled to my silence. About her business, her identity. But the truth of what Randall kept saying was hard to deny. I couldn't make myself believe that these other killings were connected with a bunch of letters. Not for a sum like twenty thousand dollars. And especially not when four known hoodlums had travelled thousands of miles. There had to be something else, something quite different. Plus, I wasn't going to be any use to Heather or anyone else, if Randall took me away. Any value I had lay in mobility.

'Did you decide to tell me?'

The rasping voice cut into my thoughts.

'I just remembered something,' I told him.

'Well, well. Ain't life full of surprises? As soon as the question of jail comes up, people remember things. Must be the smell of the disinfectant. Just leave out the fairy tale this time. Else I swear, I'll throw a conspiracy rap at you. Jointly with Hans Christian Andersen.'

I didn't really pay him much attention. My mind was too busy, racing ahead to what I could safely tell him, without having him charge me with any one of half a dozen offences.

'To start with, that story about the letters — '

' — Aha — '

' — is true.'

Snort of disbelief. Then,

'Remember what I told you.'

'I'm remembering. It's still true. What I forgot to mention was that when I reached Barnes' house, there were other people there. Three men. No, four.'

'Make up your mind,' he advised nastily.

'It turned out to be four. I think the three I saw first were your men from back East. The boss was a short, heavy-set character with a face like chopped liver — '

'Manny Levers — ' intoned Randall.

' — there was another one, a real nasty character they called Shortie — '

' — Shortie Jack Becker.'

' — and a third man. He grinned a lot. Loud dresser.'

'Peter Hooper. They call him Bright-Eyes Hooper. He's the one who's unaccounted for. So what happened? Who did Barnes say these guys were?'

The curved ball. But I was ready for it. I could not pretend Barnes had been alive at the time. The autopsy report would tell a different story. And I couldn't say he was dead. That would make me a guy who failed to report a murder. The police officer hasn't been born who'd let me get away with that one.

'Barnes wasn't around. These three characters waved guns at me, acted tough. I wasn't expecting them, or anybody like them. Blackmail is a one-man operation as a rule. Two people at most. As you said just now, it's the wrong field entirely for people like that.'

'So why did they get tough?' he demanded.

Then I had an inspiration.

'They thought I might be Barnes.'

'Why would they think that?'

'It was Barnes' house. I suppose if you don't know what a man looks like, it's reasonable to assume that somebody who turns up at his house is the man you want.'

'Maybe,' he shrugged, non-commitally. 'Then what?'

'They didn't like me much. But they could see I was harmless. They growled and scratched for a while, then they had to leave. Some kind of appointment that wouldn't wait. They told me to let Barnes know they were looking for him.'

'What name did they give?'

'No names. They said he would know who it was. They told me to stay there fifteen minutes, then they left. I was watching them through the window, when suddenly I got slugged from behind. That was the first time I knew there was another man.'

His face brightened a little.

'Slugged, you say? But that would leave a bruise, wouldn't it?'

I was safe enough on that one.

'You'd better believe it,' I confirmed, sliding rueful fingers around the back of my head, and turning away from him. 'Can you see it?'

'No. And I'm not getting up twice. I'll feel it before I leave.'

That was the most hopeful thing he'd said so far. He said 'I leave'. Not 'we leave'. He was still talking.

'Why didn't you report this to the police? You say you were threatened with a gun, struck on the head.'

But I could answer that with confidence.

'C'm on Gil. You're not being serious. This is the kind of thinking people do after the event. Can you imagine the reaction I would get, if I reported stuff like that? A nasty man was rude to me, another man hit me. They'd probably give me a woman officer to make sure I got home safe.'

Randall was in no mood for grinning, but there was an extra light in his eyes.

'Just the same, it would have been the right thing to do. This guy who slugged you. You think it was Barnes?'

'It could have been, but I doubt it. If Barnes had been around, even if he'd been hiding from those other characters, he'd have at least wanted to know what I was doing there. Plenty of time for slugging after that, if it was still in his mind.'

'H'm. And the bad men didn't give you a hint what they were doing there?'

'Nothing.'

Then he shifted his ground.

'The way you tell it, your client becomes our number one suspect.'

'You have to be kidding,' I protested.

'Not on the department's time. People who get blackmailed have been known to bump off the blackmailers.'

'True. But they don't go around rubbing out every mobster in sight.'

'Maybe not. Let's just deal with one killing at a time. Did those letters turn up?'

'Not so far.'

He stood up, blocking out most of the light.

'Do I have to apply for a court order to

159

get the name of this mysterious countess?'

That jail door was still too close at hand for me to play games.

'I'll tell you the truth, Gil. This is getting out of hand. Blackmail, a little pressure here and there, that's one thing. Multiple murder, like this, is something else entirely. I'm not going up against the organisation for a few hundred dollars. Give me a few hours. I'll tell my client I'm going to have to duck this one, no charge. I will advise her to contact the department.'

'And if she doesn't? By, say, midnight tonight?'

'Then I'll tell you myself.'

He stood there, pondering.

'Midnight?'

'I guarantee it.'

'And meantime, if you stumble across anything that might be of use to a poor police officer, you'll report in?'

I put a hand on my heart.

'So help me.'

'H'm.' He leaned over. 'Where's this famous bruise?'

I turned the back of my head towards

him, winced as the sausage fingers located the tenderness. He chuckled.

'I'll say one thing for you, Preston. When you go into the bruise business, it's king-size or nothing.'

'Just hope I get a chance to return the favour.'

He paused at the doorway.

'Midnight,' he stated flatly.

10

I called Heather Dentman. She replied quickly, like someone who was sitting by the phone, waiting.

'It's me, Preston.'

'Thank Heavens you called. I was getting spooked up here by myself.'

'Then it's time you got out, for a break. We have to talk. A lot of things have been happening.'

Her voice was anxious.

'What things?'

I ignored that.

'There's a hamburger stand up on Indian Point. You probably know the one.'

'I've seen it, yes. But why don't you come here? I mean, suppose there's a call?'

'I can't come there right now. There are reasons. I'll explain when I see you. Fifteen minutes?'

'If you think it's absolutely necessary.'

'See you there.'

I hung up on that puzzled and anxious voice, and went through to the outer office.

'Florence, I want you to get hold of Sam Thompson.'

She was already reaching for her pencil.

'What does he have to do?'

'I want him to sit right here, and look at your pretty hair. Of course, I don't guarantee he'll stop at your hair. You know the way Sam is. But a girl has to live with that kind of stuff.'

A Digby sniff is a sniff to remember.

'I can handle Sam Thompson. But what is it you really want him to do?'

'I really want him to sit here. Kind of keep you company. I seem to be getting involved in some heavy action. The trouble is, I don't know what it's all about, or the names of all the other players. But people seem to know about me. Might even decide to pay me a little call.'

Her face was quite composed, as she asked,

'You mean Sam will be here to protect me?'

'Call it insurance.'

'H'm. Wouldn't it be cheaper just to send me home?'

Good old Florence. Always nagging at me to keep down the costs.

'Cheaper maybe, but not efficient. And don't worry. I'm not expecting a platoon of mugs with machine guns. I'm not really expecting anybody at all. Like I say, it's just insurance. And I don't want the telephone unmanned. I would guess the chances of a telephone call are stronger than a personal visit. Better use the tape machine the rest of the day. Just could be a voice you don't recognise that I might know when I hear the recording.'

'Very well. It all sounds very dramatic.'

She paused enquiringly, in that way she has when I'm being invited to fill in the empty spaces. Some invitations can be refused.

'If I'm not back here before then, just lock up the store as usual, will you?'

'Should I tell my bodyguard to report in the morning?'

'That might not be such a dumb idea. Can't be too careful.'

'I suppose it's no use asking for a number where I can reach you?'

'That's right, it isn't. And not because I'm being coy. I'm just out following my nose. If I settle down anywhere for any length of time, I'll call in. Meantime, Thompson.'

She was already dialling when I closed the door.

I drove steadily through thinning traffic as the road wound upwards towards Indian Point. It is one of the spots marked in our tourist leaflets, a sudden outcropping of rock at the head of a cliff. The wind and the rain have taken their toll over the centuries, until even a person with little imagination could make it into the rough outline of an Indian, hawk-nose, feathers and all. People of a more fanciful turn of mind prefer to go up there on a night of bright moonlight, when the softer glow gives even more reality to the image. Some even claim to hear the music of an Indian pipe, coming over the crashing noises of the waves, hundreds of feet below. Less romantic souls attribute the so-called music to the sea-breeze, finding its way through a series of holes in the rock. Not that the Point is just a pretty face. The wind can be very unpredictable on the more exposed areas. Every year, two or three people get caught out unexpectedly by sudden gusts, particularly at night. In the morning somebody has to scrape them off the bottom.

I found the usual forty or fifty cars parked anyhow close to the summit, and left the Chev in a spot sheltered partly against the sun and the wind. There was no sign of Heather Dentman among the scattered groups of figures standing around in that aimless way people do at tourist attractions. What do they expect to happen, anyway? It's just a lump of rock, sea-view attached. Maybe they hope secretly the old Indian will let out a war-whoop. He never does.

The breeze dropped for a brief moment, and in that moment a sharp smell hit my nostrils.

'Onions, right?' enquired my stomach.

'So?'

'So how about putting me to work? It's

been a long time.'

The hamburger man looked at me expectantly.

'King-size or regular?'

'Reg — King-size,' I amended.

'With onions,' reminded Stomach.

'With onions. And mustard too,' I added hastily, before there were more interruptions from my rebellious middle.

I paid the man, and bit into those savoury smells. Stomach was right. It had been a long time since we worked together.

'If this is an invitation to a late lunch, no thank you. I don't eat in the middle of the day.'

Heather Dentman's voice sounded over my shoulder. I turned around, caught in the act.

'Sorry about this,' I chewed. 'Been too busy chasing around.'

'You'll get fat.'

I took one more huge bite, shrugged an apology, dumped the rest in a litter bin and took a look at her.

She'd changed outfits since morning. A gray suit of light tweed was now doing its best to make her look severe, but the designer has yet to be born who could hope to deceive anybody about the Dentman shape. A knife-edge of breeze through my thin jacket reminded me that, summer or no, this was still the Point.

I walked beside her to where we had a clear view out across the ocean, and nobody within twenty yards.

'Why wouldn't you come to the apartment?' she queried. 'There's no wind, and the food's better.'

'Security,' I told her. 'And I mean that literally. Your manager, Hackett, takes too much interest in your welfare. Or maybe you knew already.'

But she hadn't known. I was watching her face.

'You'll have to explain that,' she admitted.

'Hackett told your husband about my last visit. Wouldn't do for old George to get any wrong ideas about our relationship. Besides, I don't like being spied on.'

'I see.'

The tone was flat. Not too interested. I had to remember that she'd had a nasty shock just a few hours earlier. Whatever the bigger moralities may have been about her relationship with Barnes, there was no doubt she'd really been stuck on the man. And was taking it all very well. So far. Now, she looked at me, without expression.

'In any case, you needn't worry too much about what George thinks. Not until tomorrow. He had to leave for San Diego this morning. Something to do with Cecile's business affairs. To be fair to her, she does keep on trying to make George feel he's important.'

'And isn't he?' I queried.

With just the ghost of a smile, she informed me,

'When you're talking about Cecile, and business matters, you have to understand that nobody else is really of any importance at all. That lady has everything sewn up tight. You should see her eating her way through a legal document. Even the lawyers pay attention. But her heart is in the right place. If it makes George feel important to buzz along to a meeting with his little brief-case, then she encourages it.'

So that was why I hadn't been able to get him on the phone. His mother was the one who paid the piper, after all. George could scarcely be expected to tell her he couldn't oblige at that time, because he was waiting for a call from a man who was trying to bust up his marriage. Or so he thought. It was a relief in a way. Whatever was going to happen, was going to happen by midnight. After that, Rourke and Randall would be in charge. Any little influence I might have on events would come to an end.

'Hey, mister.'

I was interrupted by a small, shrill voice. Turning, I saw a little boy waving at me and pointing. Two yards away, an orange ball had come to rest. I stepped across and kicked it back to him.

'Thanks,' he called.

Heather watched impassively.

'We didn't come up here to play ball, I imagine?'

'Not unless it has a large figure eight stamped on it,' I agreed. 'Did you notice?'

'Figure eight?' she repeated. 'Isn't that

something to do with pool?'

'Something,' I agreed. 'The eight-ball can be very bad news. If you get stuck behind it.'

'And are we?'

'I think we might be.'

In the distance, my ball-partner was moving away with his friends. He waved at me. I raised an arm in reply.

'I don't want to sound stuffy,' Heather assured me. 'But if we are to communicate, it'll have to be in English. My pool-room is somewhat rusty.'

'Sorry about that.' I was trying to get my thoughts in order. 'I told you over the phone that things have been happening. Things which are going to be out of my hands a few hours from now.'

She wasn't one to wring her hands and fret. She just waited. I told her about the people I'd found at Barnes' house, who they were and what had happened since. The business about the fire brought a shudder from her otherwise calm face. Earl Gannon I kept till the end.

'What is really bugging the police is the gun that was used to kill Barnes. Because that same gun was used just a few days ago. To eliminate a hoodlum. From the same part of the world as my three friends. His name was Earl Gannon.'

I was watching her expression as I suddenly produced the name. There seemed to be a reaction of some kind.

'Did you know him, this Gannon?'

Heather shook her head.

'No. But that name. It isn't very ordinary, is it. And I'm sure I've heard it recently. I remember thinking it was rather unusual.'

'When did you hear it, Heather? Where were you at the time? Who were you talking to?'

I hardly dared to think I might be going to get a break.

'I'm sure it was something to do with Clive. Wait a minute. Let me think.'

I let her think. She stood quite still, staring at the ground for long seconds. It would have been a comfort to know whether she was trying to remember, or simply trying to think up a good yarn for my benefit.

'The sister,' she muttered, half to

herself. Then, giving me her attention again, 'yes, that was it. Clive's sister. The one who lives in Sacramento. Her married name is Gannon.'

'Ah.'

I let out a long breath of satisfaction.

'Did you ever meet her?'

'No. I understood she'd left her husband, several months ago now, and was making a new life for herself away from him.'

'Were she and Clive close, would you say?'

'I would say they had a good relationship, yes. He always spoke fondly of her.'

I stood, with my back to the wind, hands cupped, snapping at my lighter until a spark found a home on tobacco.

'So what's the possibility?' I pondered. 'Let's assume our man Gannon was the sister's husband. If that's true, there are all kinds of reasons for him to visit Clive Barnes.'

'Many,' she agreed. 'Particularly in the circumstances.'

'Circumstances?'

'Yes, the fact that she'd left him. He might have wanted Clive to help him get her back.'

'Or tell him where she was living, maybe.'

'Or blame him for the separation.'

'Or — ' I stopped, and grinned. 'I think we've covered enough ground already to justify what you said. All kinds of reasons. We could go on guessing for hours.'

Heather looked at me as though she wanted to say something, but was uncertain of her reception.

'You have a theory?' I prompted.

'Just a thought. If Gannon was some kind of criminal, is it too obvious to suggest that these other men followed him here, and killed him? And then — and then killed Clive, because he'd found out something about it? You said the same gun was used.'

I tried not to put her down too hard.

'No, that isn't at all crazy. In fact, it would have been the most logical way to work this thing out. But it won't do, Heather. Those guys were thousands of miles away when Gannon got hit. The

174

thinking is that they came here to find out what happened.'

'I see. Then we're no further forward.' She sounded downcast.

'Wrong,' I contradicted. 'This information about Barnes' sister, it explains a lot. For instance, it tells us why he seemed to get himself involved suddenly with a bunch of underworld people. An accident of marriage. That particular institution has led a lot of people into some very strange situations.'

I had only meant to give her ego a boost. She winced.

'Ouch.'

'It gives me something else to look into,' I continued hurriedly. 'The trouble is, there isn't much time.'

'Time? Oh yes, you said something about only a few hours.'

This was the part I'd been delaying as long as I could.

'The police are all over me. They have a fistful of charges they can make, and they will very soon, if I don't co-operate. I have until midnight. Then I have to tell them who you are.'

There was no point in trying to soften the blow.

'Tell them who — ?' There was alarm on her face, and in her voice. 'But I'm your client. I thought the law protected me in that situation. And in any case, none of all this terrible business is any of my concern.'

'I know that,' I soothed, hoping I believed it, 'but it just doesn't change anything, not from where the police stand. Four people are dead. You were involved with one of them. Heavily involved. From a police point of view, you even had a motive to kill Clive Barnes, yourself.'

Her face was shocked.

'Do you believe that?'

'No, I don't. But I'm not the police. They know you exist, they know you are involved. It isn't enough for them to have me tell them you didn't murder Barnes. They have to talk to you themselves.'

'Is there no alternative?' she pleaded.

'Oh yes,' I admitted. 'The alternative is they put me behind bars. Then they get a court order, instructing me to divulge the identity of my client. Even then, I don't have to tell them. I get convicted of contempt of court, and draw a minimum of sixty days in the cooler. Plus — ' as I could see she was about to interrupt — 'they will revoke my licence. I will be out of a job. And that means permanently.'

'I see. So everything will come out now. It won't be any longer merely a question of keeping Cecile from finding out. The whole thing will be spread all over every cheap newspaper on the coast.'

'No.'

I rapped out the negative with more authority than I could reasonably justify. It seemed to restore a little hope to her crumbling features.

'No,' I repeated, more gently. 'The police are not out to persecute people. They're only interested in finding out who did what. The officers in charge of the case are old friends of mine — '

'You just said they'd send you to jail,' she contradicted.

'I did. And they will, if I don't play straight. Nobody has any friends in a case of multiple murder. But if I stick to the rules, tell them your story, it'll probably remain confidential. If they wanted, they could fill the newspapers every day. That isn't their job, and it isn't what they do. Once they've talked with you, satisfied themselves, they'll leave you alone.'

'You really believe that?'

'I know it. I've worked with them many times. It's only because of our long association they've agreed to leave me walking around until midnight.'

She looked sceptical.

'You don't really expect to find out anything by then?'

I shrugged.

'Maybe not. But this is murder we're talking about. Somewhere around this city there's a killer. He's nervous. Watching, waiting. We've already seen how fast he can move. As soon as those three characters began to get close, he acted. This is a minute by minute situation we have here. Plenty can happen by midnight.'

'But what will you do?'

'I have a few people to see, places to go.

And whether or not there was a connection between these killings and your missing letters when we started, there is now. I'm still hoping you'll get that blackmail call. If the two things go together, twenty thousand dollars is a nice round sum to have in your pocket, if you need a fast airplane ticket.'

She nodded absently, pulling her jacket closer round her shoulders against the stiffening breeze.

'So I just go home and wait again?'

'I'm afraid so. And, by the way, take it easy when that man Hackett is around. Whatever he finds out goes straight to your husband.'

'I hate to be spied on, too. I'll remember.'

I walked back with her to where she'd left her car. As she unlocked the door, I pressed her arm encouragingly.

'I know you must feel the world is coming to an end,' I said gently. 'But it isn't, you know. I've been here before. Many times. We'll get you through this.'

'We?' she queried.

'Certainly we. Me, for one. And you.

Something tells me they don't give up so easily, where you come from.'

A faint smile.

'Thank you. I know you'll do what you can.'

I watched her out of sight, then went back to my own car, deep in thought.

Naturally, I'll do what I can, I was thinking.

But what was there?

11

'You looking for Charlie?'

I stopped banging on the door, and looked round at the voice. A man stood, peering out from the next door along the passage. Sixty plus, with a gray shave, blue suspenders over a grimy undervest. Eyeglasses perched crookedly on the red and purple nose. Blackened toes peeped coyly from the bottoms of stained blue serge pants. If he had an appointment for dinner at the Monkton Hilton, he wasn't entirely dressed for it yet.

'That's right,' I told him.

'Whaddya want with him? You some kind of collector from the finance house?'

It was on the tip of my tongue to tell him to go peddle his hygiene pills, when I reminded myself that elderly neighbours can be mines of information.

'Wrong way round, pop,' I grinned. 'I'm the goodnews man. Old Charlie got lucky today. His number came up.'

'No kidding? You're the pay-off man?'

The slack face dropped even further. I shook my head.

'Oh no. That isn't the way it's done. I just make the contact. Be sure I have the right party. Then the party and me talk about the details. We fix some safe way to get the money to him. You know, it's a terrible thing, back in the old days guys like me could actually carry the money around. The bad guys would take it away from us, so the winning party never did collect. Not any more. Today we got system.'

His thumb was making a rasping noise on the white chin-stubble.

'Imagine,' he muttered. 'Old Charlie. And him my best buddy.'

I'll say one thing for the people who get the right number. They're always very nice people. They have to be, judging by the crowds of best buddies they turn out to have. I banged at the door again.

'You're wasting your time,' he advised. 'Charlie ain't here.'

'Oh? I thought he would be. We already called at the tennis club where he works.

182

They told us he called in sick.'

'I don't know nothing about that,' he said stubbornly. 'All I know, he woke me up this morning, told me he had to go away for a coupla days.'

'What time was that?'

'Time? Hell, I don't know. I was getting ready for bed. Maybe eight-thirty. Nine o'clock.'

'Ready for bed?' I queried.

'Yeah. I'm a night guard, you know. Security patrol.'

It figured. Makes a man feel safe at night, knowing the dark hours are being policed by alert and vigorous men like Charlie's best buddy.

'Did he say where he was going? Did he leave a phone number where I might catch him?'

The grimy head moved in denial.

'No. He seemed kind of excited. Say, you don't imagine he knew about the prize, huh? Went off to hide? Some people would do that, you know. Some people get awful close if they win a few bucks. Even with their old pals. There was a guy I knew one time — '

183

'No,' I interrupted. 'He couldn't have known. This is today's numbers we're talking about. This is too bad. I hope Charlie isn't gonna break the rules.'

'Rules?'

'Certainly. If we can't make some kind of contact within twenty-four hours, then we have no proof of identity. The prize stays in the pot.'

Alarm now.

'But that's terrible. You people can't do that to old Charlie. He won that money fair and square.'

'And he'll be paid, if we can find him. Are you positive you can't think of any place he could have gone?'

He was thinking hard, screwing up his face with the pain of stirring up all that dusty machinery inside his head.

'Was he carrying a bag of any kind? I mean like a suitcase?'

'Now you bring it up, he did have a case with him. Like he was going to stay some place, you know?'

It was no use. I'd been hoping that Charlie might have been able to give me some information about Barnes' recent callers at the club. A locker-room attendant is not the most over-worked man in the world. He would have had plenty of time to observe little comings and goings at the club. Now he'd moved on, destination unknown. And I was running out of time. I scribbled on a piece of paper, held it out to my informant.

'If he comes back, have him call this number.'

He squinted at it, making a face.

'Parkside number,' he whistled. 'Charlie really hit the big-time, huh?'

'I told you. Now don't forget. And if you come up with an idea, anything at all, you use that number. There'll be another ten bucks in it for you, pop.'

'Another ten bucks?' he questioned.

'Right. To keep company with this one.'

I passed him a folded ten-spot. Bony fingers clamped around it.

'I'll sure be thinking hard, mister.'

Back out on the street, I spotted a pay-phone that wasn't occupied. Sam Thompson's voice sounded at the other end.

'Preston Investigations.'

'It's me, Sam. Why doesn't Florence answer?'

'Oh, hi. She had to go out. Pick up some drycleaning or something. What's going on?'

'I called to ask you that,' I told him.

'Oh. Yeah. Well, nothing. This is the easiest money I ever earned. If you need me here permanent, I'll be glad to — '

'Nobody's been in the office?' I interrupted.

'No.'

'How about calls?'

Thompson is very strong in some departments. Office routine is not one of them.

'Calls. Yes, that's right. There was a call a few minutes ago. Our Miss Digby seemed all excited. Wrote it down some place. Hold the phone, will you?'

I stared out at the business traffic, picking up now as the earlier offices and shops ceased trading for the day. The snarl would worsen gradually for the next hour, then thin away again.

'Preston?'

186

'I'm here.'

'Got that note. It says Mrs. Dentman wants to see you right away. Urgent, it says.'

'I'm on my way,' I snapped.

'Hold it. Don't you want to know where?'

About to tell him I knew where, I changed my mind.

'O.K. Where?'

'At the del Pacifico.'

'In one of the bars, or what? Does it say?'

'Will you let me read this thing? No bars. She'll be in Suite 27A.'

It made no sense. Thompson was right. I ought to stop interrupting him.

'You better read the whole thing, Sam.'

'I just did. That's it.'

'Florence usually notes the time of a call.'

'Correct. It was twenty minutes ago.'

'Better keep the note. Florence likes to be tidy. Tell her you gave me the message.'

'The time, too?'

'The time, too.'

Thoughtfully, I put down the phone,

drumming my fingers on a tattered city directory. It was little more than an hour since I'd sent Heather back to her own apartment. And yet, according to Florence's note, forty minutes later she was installed in a suite at one of the most expensive hotels in town. A familiar tingling sensation was beginning to work at the back of my neck. Something was going to break, at last.

'Hey, man.'

An irritable voice came muffled through the glass of the booth. A man stood scowling at me. I pushed open the door.

'You wanna place to sleep, we got hotels, you know?'

I winked at him.

'You're right. Think I'll go to one.'

He snorted, pushing past me through the door.

★   ★   ★

The Hotel del Pacifico is the twentieth century equivalent of the old-style end-of-trail saloon. A big welcome for the weary traveller, then a fast programme of food, booze, hot baths, maybe a little entertainment, if the nuggets in the old poke will run to it. A couple of days on the treatment, and the traveller finds himself outside, blinking contentedly in the sun. Almost as weary as when he came, but happier now, and at least no longer troubled by having to carry all that gold around. He has had something called A Good Time, whatever that may be.

The strained and anxious man who checks in these days, does not leave a gaunt and used-up horse tethered outside. The only horses he has knowledge of are the ones which let him down regularly on the question of passing the post. He has not reached his destination by surviving the desert, the Indians, the rattlesnakes. His trail has been strewn with sales trends, market downswings, computer soft-ware, elusive targets, and the unpredictable caprice of a distant master called Wall Street. He is known as a delegate. He has come to meet a lot of other men, at a gathering called a convention. Here he will be scolded, praised, raised up, cast down, reminded of past sins, forgiven. Harangued by sad-eyed bitter men, with angry diagrams and charts of lost opportunities. Exalted by bright-eyed, confident men, with colourful maps of the way ahead, the new gold-trails to be blazed. And perhaps, who could tell, even a confidential nudge from J.S.B. himself.

Throughout all this will run a continual stream of food, booze and entertainment, just like always. There will be plenty to tell Martha and the kids when he gets back. And maybe a few little items best not reported. Like that little dark item last year, you remember the one. She did this dance — ?

I threaded my way to the reception desk through a stream of excited, chattering men with papers folded under their arms. From the scraps of conversation I heard, next year was going to be different.

An immaculate character looked me over with a detached air of anything-we-can-do.

'I have an appointment. Suite 27A. My

name is Preston.'

His hand moved automatically to a clip-board, with notes trapped under the steel.

'Ah yes, Mrs. Dentman left word. Will you please go right up, Mr. Preston? Second floor, to your right.'

I nodded my thanks, walking across to the elevators, and deciding against it when I saw the waiting mob. The staircase was wide, and heavily carpeted. The downstairs noise and bustle faded quickly away, before the almost monastic silence of the upper floors. Maybe monastic would be the wrong word, I thought, as I caught a distant glimpse of a woman disappearing through a doorway.

Suite 27A had nothing to tell me from outside. Except that it was identical in appearance to 26A on the left, and 28A on the right. I leaned on the button, wondering.

The door opened quickly. A man stood there. He was fifty plus, with flat gray hair and a face like slate, with small black eyes glittering in their recesses. Somebody hadn't liked the way his nose was set, so they'd moved it slightly to one side at some time in the past. An ex-fighter?

'You're Preston, right?'

'Right.'

He didn't offer his own name, but stood to one side to let me enter. There was that uncomfortable feeling about him, that made me glad I was carrying company in the shape of the .38. It was a small relief when he decided to lead the way.

'In here.'

I followed him out of the little hallway, where two other doors led off, and into a room large enough to hold a small meeting. There was a woman sitting on a high-back chair, watching us come in. She wore a floor-length, form-fitting dress of red silk over the shape of a twenty-year old girl. Her hair was pure white and swept up in immaculate waves to form gleaming rolls at the top of her head. But it was the face that made the impact. I'd seen it on statues of Greek goddesses. Serene, untrammelled, beautiful. In the violet eyes there was amusement as she saw me drinking her in. She'd seen men look at her that way for years. How many years? Thirty-five? Forty? I couldn't tell.

The man who'd let me in had moved to one side, and stood there, unspeaking. I dug my voice out from somewhere.

'I was expecting to see Mrs. Dentman.'

It sounded ungrateful, considering the substitute. The sculptured head inclined slightly.

'I am Mrs. Dentman.'

I was so enteranced with the musical voice that I didn't absorb the words for a full five seconds. Then I began to function again. Mrs. Dentman. Cecile Dentman. This had to be George's mother. But it wasn't possible. No. George was thirty years old. That would make her at least — No. No. There had to be some mistake.

'Forgive me,' I stumbled, 'but the only Mrs. Dentman I know is Heather Dentman. That would have to make you — '

' — her mother-in-law? Yes, it would. George Dentman is my son.'

'But, but — ' I contradicted.

She sat quite still, smiling faintly. The

man chuckled. A low, unmusical noise.

'Ridiculous, ain't it?' he demanded. 'That's what I always tell her. Cecile, I say — '

'That will do, Frank.'

The words were gentle enough, but the command unmistakable. Frank subsided at once. I remembered that I'd been in the middle of saying something.

'I was only trying to say that I'd expected Mrs. Dentman senior to be a much older lady.'

'Shawls?' she taunted. 'A little bead-work perhaps?'

I didn't shuffle my feet, but the effect was the same.

'Well — er — no,' I denied. 'That is, whatever I expected, it certainly wasn't you.'

'You're disappointed?'

By saying that, she broke the spell. It made her just another good-looking woman playing with a man. And I've been played with before.

'I find old ladies in shawls easier to push around,' I told her. 'What's this all about, Mrs. Dentman?'

She made a little face of disappointment. She'd been enjoying the game. Now she waved an arm.

'Please sit down, Mr. Preston. There.'

I sat where she pointed, half-expecting that Frank would sit down with us. He stayed where he was. This latest development was so unexpected that my mind was protesting at all the double-speed thinking now demanded. I had no way of judging what these two would be tossing in my direction. What they knew, what they suspected, what they wanted with me, these were all wide-open areas. But the over-riding factor so far as I was concerned was a simple one. This whole business had started, for me at least, because Heather Dentman had been misbehaving herself, and could not afford to have her mother-in-law know. So much had happened since, so many other people had become involved, that the question of a little side-order blackmail was little more than one item in a whole bag of items. The sign on the bag read 'Murder'. But my client was still Heather, and this groomed woman was just as large in her life as ever. George's life, too, of course, I mustn't overlook old George. In a twisted way, I was looking after his interests, too.

'You're probably wondering about Mr. Dee.'

That voice was always going to be a pleasure to hear, even if the sentiments became unwelcome.

'Who?'

'That's me,' gritted Frank.

I hadn't given him much thought at all, until then.

'Well, not exactly — ' I demurred.

'Mr. Dee is an old and trusted friend. He takes care of me. What was that title we agreed, Frank, personal secretary?'

'Huh,' he snorted. 'What she means is, I do all the work.'

I nodded, as though I understood.

'Mr. Dee used to work for my husband, before I lost him, and it just seemed natural for him to carry right on. We've been together so many years now, I sometimes find it difficult to remember who is supposed to work for who.'

She smiled graciously at the small lie.

Around this one, there was never going to be any doubt about who was in charge. You could feel power radiating from her.

Gently I said,

'So Mr. Dee is present at all your meetings, if I understand you?'

Cecile narrowed her eyes fractionally.

'Most,' she agreed. 'Nearly all, in fact. But not quite.'

'I see. Well, now that I know about Mr. Dee, and what he's doing here, could I ask the same question about me? What am I doing here, Mrs. Dentman?'

Finely-etched eyebrows elevated, one quarter-inch.

'That, if I may say so, is a fairly naïve question. Someone who gets heavily involved in a family's private life, can scarcely be surprised if the head of that family shows interest.'

We were getting to it now. I reminded myself that this beautiful creature was a tough operator, despite the perfume. And there was always Mr. Dee. In his case, the reminder was not necessary.

'Mrs. Dentman,' I replied, very politely, 'this meeting is not my idea. You made the appointment. All I did was keep it, and not with the person I expected. That makes you the chairman of the board. And the chairman is the one who decides the business.'

'You're impudent,' she said evenly.

I shrugged, and kept quiet.

'Very well. Frank, I think you ought to take a break for a few minutes. Go and have a drink, or something. I hear that one of those bars downstairs is topless.'

Frank stayed where he was.

'I don't know,' he demurred. 'Leaving you alone with this guy may not be such a good idea.'

When she spoke, there was new steel in the voice.

'Mr. Preston will do me no harm. This is not a business matter, Frank. My family is involved here, and you know that is very much my private affair.'

Still he didn't budge.

'He has a gun,' he said stubbornly.

'I noticed that,' she agreed. To my surprise, 'You're not thinking of shooting me, are you Mr. Preston?'

'No,' I assured her. 'I almost never shoot anybody at this time of evening. It spoils my appetite.'

'There you are, Frank. I shall be quite safe. Now, off you go.'

And off he went. Reluctantly, and muttering under his breath, but he went. When the outer door clicked, we both relaxed.

'Do you mind if I smoke?'

'Please do. I like to see a man smoke. In some odd way, I find it reassuring.'

I fiddled around with a pack of Old Favorites, lit one, and looked around for an ashtray.

'Here.'

She stood up, and walked rhythmically across to a walnut table by the window. Turning, she came across to me, leaning down, and putting a glass ashtray where I could reach it. It was a small enough act, but significant. Cecile Dentman had stirred out of her chair to perform a small service for a guest. She could just as easily have pointed out to me what I wanted and let me do my own carrying. A gesture, indeed.

And now she was leaning beside me, one slender arm setting the ashtray just so, the smell of her all around me, the sheer physical presence almost aggressive. I didn't stir a muscle, until she went away and resumed her seat. Then I managed a strangled,

'Thank you.'

She knew what she'd done, and was enjoying it.

'Very good, Mr. Preston.'

'Howzat?'

But I knew what she meant. And she was aware of it.

'I think you know. Nine men out of ten would have made some kind of grab at me. A woman is always more intrigued by number ten.'

I nodded foolishly, wondering when the chairman of the board would get down to business.

'You know what Groucho said once. A woman is only a woman, but an Old Favorite is a cigarette.'

She licked appreciatively at one corner of the red mouth. It would have been a pleasure to offer some assistance.

'That isn't what he said, and it wasn't even Groucho. Now, let us talk.'

I nodded my head, to show I was listening.

'I am not one to relish publicity,' she began. 'I keep myself out of the public gaze. Indeed, I don't believe you will find even one photograph of me in any local newspaper. Privacy is my watchword. That is what I pay for, that is what I get. So far as is humanly possible, I expect the same kind of behaviour from those who depend on me. You find that unreasonable?'

'Not a bit,' he told her. 'The one who pays the piper, and so forth.'

'Exactly. Naturally, I'm always interested in the comings and goings of my family, just as anyone is. But in my case, I take perhaps rather a closer look than most people. I have to be on guard, you understand, on the lookout for events, people, anything that could bring some unwelcome attention. It would seem that you might come into this category.'

She looked over, waiting for some contribution.

I returned her gaze steadily.

'Would I be classified as an event, or a people?'

Those eyes became less than friendly.

'I have no doubt your brand of humor is a tremendous success with dance-hall girls and waitresses. Please spare me of it. To stick to the facts, you appear to have arrived very positively onto my family scene. Or perhaps erupted would be more apt.'

I tapped ash with great care.

'You'll have to be more specific, lady.'

'Very well, then. Specifically, you paid a call on my daughter-in-law yesterday afternoon.'

'It seems everyone in town knows about that,' I grouched.

'It's no mystery. No one goes in or out of that block without my knowledge. I'm part-owner of the place.'

Hackett again, I thought savagely. The so-called manager was a one-man information bureau. He probably carried the television news concession as well.

'Very well, so I was there. What of it?'

'I would very much like to know what

you and Heather talked about,' she told me softly.

'Then why don't you ask her?' I suggested.

'You won't tell me?'

'Mrs. Dentman, I am in a confidential business.' I even kept my tone smooth. 'How would it look if I went around blabbing about the business of the people who employ me?'

Quick as a flash, she shot out,

'So you admit she employed you?'

'I admit nothing. I'm not on trial here.'

But it was beginning to feel that way.

'My son thinks Heather is having him followed,' she continued calmly. 'He suspects that's why she hired you.'

'Is that why you packed him off so fast?'

I wasn't going to crack her composure that easily. But there was just an extra edge to her voice now.

'George had an important meeting to attend.'

'Huh,' I scoffed. 'Couldn't have happened at a more convenient time, could it? I mean, the very day momma is going to buy off the nasty detective. That's why I'm here, isn't it? To be bought off?'

The splendid breasts rose a little higher than usual, as she took a deep breath.

'When people pretend they're not interested in money, it usually means they are either cranks or liars. You don't strike me as being a crank, Mr. Preston.'

Which seemed to narrow the options.

'You left out a category,' I pointed out. 'Some people just don't want to sell.'

Again that faint smile.

'This information is so valuable?' she queried. 'A secret beyond price? Is that why you can't sell?'

'No. You misunderstand. The thing which isn't for sale is me. I may not be much, but I'm all I have. And I'm not for sale, Mrs. Dentman. Now we understand each other, I'll be on my way.'

I began to get up.

'Sit down.'

The words were like a coiled whip snaking through the air between us. I found myself sitting again, as though I'd been struck.

'We're going to have to dispense with a

few formalities, Preston.'

Like the formality of calling me 'Mr.'. We seemed to have dispensed with that one already.

'Since we're getting informal, let me tell you something, Cecile,' and I noted the wince, 'I know your kind, and I've met you before, and you don't scare me. You've got ten zillion dollars, and you decide who's going to be President, and my licence isn't worth the paper it's written on, and you can get me hounded out of every state in the union. You're a very tough lady, and when you shout, people jump. Or else. There's a phone behind you. Call up the governor, and the police commissioner, and a few others.'

'You think I couldn't do it?' she snapped.

'Break me? It's possible,' I shrugged. 'But you don't buy me.'

She folded her hands together, white-knuckled, while she controlled her temper. After a few more deep breaths, she said, in a conversational tone,

'You almost made me let fly, then. Not many people can do that, not these days.

You're a man to be watched.'

'I'm being watched, the way you tell it,' I replied ungraciously. 'It seems every newsboy in town is on the payroll.'

'Not quite. However, I have learned one or two things about you lately. Things which will not help me sleep more easily. Did you watch High Noon-time today?'

That's the name of a mid-day news and people round-up on our local tee-vee station.

'No.'

'It seems there was a fire in which two people died. The reports claimed that among those early on the scene was the well-known private investigator, Mark Preston.'

She waited for a reaction. I shrugged.

'I was just passing by. They have to grab whatever they can get to fill up those thirty minutes.'

'You have a habit of just passing by,' she continued. 'Last night you were passing by when a man named Clive Barnes died. Only he was murdered.'

'Coincidence.'

'And you happened to pass him by just

a few hours after you left my daughter-in-law. She and this Barnes have been sleeping together. Stretching coincidence rather hard, wouldn't you say?'

Ouch. That one came up from the floor. For the moment, I was mentally dazed. The whole need for Heather to employ me had arisen because she was afraid some letters might reach this female bastion of purity. Now it all seemed futile, unnecessary. Cecile had known about Barnes all along. I floundered around, looking for understanding.

'You haven't answered me,' she pressed.

'I don't know what you want me to say,' I mumbled. 'Your daughter-in-law's private life is no concern of mine.'

The weakness of my reply brought contempt to her face.

'I think you made it your business,' she said bleakly. 'I think Heather called you in because Barnes was making himself a nuisance. Over money, at a guess. It usually is. I further think that you went to see Barnes to strongarm the man. Things got out of hand, and you killed him.'

I wished she'd stop hammering at me,

so I could get my thoughts straightened out.

'That's ridiculous.'

'I don't think so. And if the police knew about Heather, they wouldn't think so either.'

That stung a bit.

'That's all you're interested in, isn't it? Keeping your precious family out of this?'

She remained quite calm.

'That would have been true before this Barnes episode. But if Heather has been the cause of a murder, I think that puts her outside my protection. She's already been unfaithful to George. Perhaps it's time we thought about a change.'

'A change?' I echoed, uncomprehending.

'Yes. My son and his wife are not exactly the match of the century. He'll soon find someone else.'

I was getting a thought. I kept pushing it away, but it kept coming right back.

'What are you saying?' I demanded. 'I'm going to be sorry I asked this, I know. But are you trying to hire me to bump off Heather Dentman?'

The laugh was genuine. Cecile had to hold her head back, to give it full rein. Late, slanting sunlight danced from the gleaming teeth.

'What a very crude creature you are. Like some animal from the jungle. No, thank you. We don't need any murders today.'

A fresh laugh broke out. I was getting sore.

'Then what are you saying?' I demanded.

She composed herself, and regarded me with eyes in which laughter had not died.

'I will deal with Heather. She will go away. There will be a quiet divorce. No fuss. I will settle money on her, and that will be the end of the matter.'

'Huh,' I snorted. 'Very tidy. And what do we do with old Clive Barnes' body? Take the slugs out, and buy him a new life? Just how much money do you have, lady?'

'Ah, yes. Mr. Barnes.'

She said it as though somebody had reminded her she left a glove in a cab.

'I want you to take responsibility for that,' she announced. 'You can plead whatever you choose. An accident, a quarrel, anything. I will provide absolutely the finest legal talent in the state for your defence. I have taken advice on the position, and I will be quite open with you. Your chance of complete acquittal is fifty-fifty. No more. If you should be convicted, the maximum term you will be required to serve is twenty two months. To compensate for this loss of freedom, I will deposit in your name, one quarter million dollars. There is only one stipulation.'

'Only one,' I muttered faintly.

'Yes. There must be no reference to me, or any member of my family at any stage of the proceedings. One reference, and our agreement is ended.'

'Ended,' I nodded.

'Well, what do you say?' she demanded.

This time I really did stand up.

'I don't think you're using your money properly, Cecile. You ought to be calling in every head-shrinker in the country. What do I say? I say you're nuts, that's what. You've been pushing people around so long your mind is scrambled. I think you're dangerous. I'm getting out of here.'

She sat very still, red spots burning in her cheeks.

'How dare you speak to me like that,' she hissed.

'Put it down to hysteria. And tell Mr. Dee I said goodbye.'

Before I reached the door she spoke again.

'If you leave here under these circumstances, you do so as my enemy, Preston. Think carefully. I make a very bad enemy.'

'Me too,' I assured her. 'And I have a very big edge over you, Cecile. I'm not a candidate for the funny farm.'

As I closed the door of Suite 27A, I was trembling.

12

I went back downstairs to the lobby, deep in thought. A new bunch of jaded pioneers was just arriving, and there was a lot of jostling and arm-punching and shouted recognition going on. I elbowed a sour path through the throng, trying to bring back something that had been said in the early part of my conversation upstairs. Something before we got stripped right off for the real wrestling match. Then I had it.

'Where's the nearest men's room?'

I spoke to a sweating man in hotel uniform who was trying to reach the desk, loaded down with about two dozen assorted bags. He jerked a head to the right. I thanked him and went away in that direction.

It was the usual layout, with a row of immaculate handbasins complete with wall-length mirror. It was the mirror I wanted. I've been toting a gun around for many years, and I'm very careful about it. Most people would have been surprised to be told that there was a hefty piece of ordnance tucked away under my jacket. But Cecile Dentman, that publicity-shy, walking Fort Knox, had spotted it instantly. Either I was getting careless, or the jacket would have to go. Even in this day and age, there are some things it doesn't pay to advertise.

I admired myself in the mirror. No bulges, nothing pulling the material out of shape. Turning sideways, I pulled my shoulders back, wriggled them from side to side. Still nothing.

Then I caught sight of a man who'd been washing his hands a couple of basins along. He'd forgotten the hands, and was watching me posturing and admiring myself. I felt foolish, and grinned at him weakly. He returned a sickly grin of his own, looked nervously around, and walked out quickly. He didn't even bother to dry his hands, and I could see his point of view.

Facing the front again, I bent forward slightly, and that was it. The material of the jacket became stretched unevenly on the side carrying the gun. There was no bulge, no outline, just this stretching effect. Most people would have noticed nothing. Even the few who registered the fact would have put it down to a fault in the tailoring. Not so, Cecile Dentman. To her it meant gun. And to me that meant a lot of years of watching out for people with guns. She was a lady full of surprises.

I went out of the hotel to get the car. At the gateway to the parking lot a young man in hotel get-up said,

'Excuse me sir, are you wanting to take your car out?'

'That was the general idea,' I admitted.

'Would you mind telling me which car is yours? Reason I ask, some of our guests have done some crazy parking in here. We're trying to get it straightened out, but there are still three cars hemmed in down there.'

I already had a feeling I was going to be one of the chosen three. I described the Chev to him.

'I'm sorry, but yes, that's one of them.

My buddy and I are pushing them around by hand. If you'd like to give me the key, I should be able to bring the car here to you in about five minutes. Ten at most.'

'Don't bother. I'll drive it myself.'

He shook his blond head.

'Sorry. The car park is hotel property. We have an arrangement with the insurance people. This jamming-up happens all the time. It's O.K. for hotel employees to move the cars around. But if anyone else is involved, and we get any damage caused, the insurance guys won't pay. Don't worry, Mac and I are good at it. You'll be out of here before you know it.'

He grinned reassuringly. I handed over the keys, and went over to lean against the railed entrance. The sun was dying fast now. Like my agreement with Randall and Rourke. In just a few hours time I'd have to —

There was a tremendous explosion, and I was flung to the ground by a great blast of air. Pieces of metal sailed over my head towards the hotel entrance. I scrambled to my feet, shaking myself like a terrier dog, and slightly dazed. People were shouting, running.

'You O.K.?' demanded a voice.

'Yeah. Yeah I think so. What — ?'

'Look.'

I followed the pointing finger to where a pall of smoke hung in what had been a parking lot, and now looked like a wrecker's yard. Cursing bitterly, I stumbled through the haze of dust and fumes towards the centre. Already, I was certain of what lay there, but I had to see. Slung across the bonnet of a ruined Packard was a rag doll figure, twisted in a grotesque travesty of a human shape. The hair was black. Beyond it was a heap of metal vaguely recognisable as my two-year-old Chevrolet. On the burning back seat was a head. The hair was blond, and where the rest of the body should have been there was one arm, and part of a steering column.

My insides began to boil. I turned away, vomiting. There were tears rolling down my face. Angry, bitter tears I could not control.

'This man needs attention.'

A crisp voice sounded somewhere to my left. Pulling myself erect I shook my head furiously.

'Police officer,' I snapped. 'Get this area cleared here. You,' pointing at a large, worried face, 'take charge till I get back. The medics are on their way, with the rest of my squad. These people will get under their feet. Get rid of 'em. Can you do it?'

'Can, and will, officer.'

He turned away, and began making official noises, herding other faces away with his arms.

I slipped away. Nobody was interested in anyone walking away from the scene. They were all too busy trying to get closer. Half a block away, I stopped. The stench was gone from my nostrils, but still I felt like hell. A flashing blue and yellow sign shouted 'Bar'. Inside I poured down a large helping of scotch, and shuddered. The men's room did not compare in every detail with the one at the Hotel del Pacifico. There was one rusting tap over a cracked basin. I used my handkerchief to wipe the sweat and grime from my face, made an attempt to straighten my tie.

That was when the fear came. The shaking began with my back, spread through my shoulders and arms. I seemed to tremble and rattle all over. It didn't last more than a few seconds. When it passed, I was soaked all over in sweat, and weak as a day-old kitten.

For the first time, I began to think about the bomb in rational terms. Somebody had been following me, waiting for the opportunity to install the device. But who? And why? I thought I could guess the why. It would have to be because the killer thought I was getting too close. All I had done was to rush all over town, asking a lot of damn-fool questions, and getting a fair proportion of lies in return. I didn't think I was any closer now than when I started, but somebody disagreed with me. Disagreed with me enough to plant four or five pounds of high explosive inside my car, and wire it up to the ignition. So there had to be something. Something I'd seen or heard which was a sight more signficant than I realised. I would have to go over everything that had happened, every conversation, remember exactly what had been said or done. It had to be there somewhere. I needed a place to think, and leaning on that cracked and dirty hand-bowl was no place to be doing it.

'A man who can't drink the stuff should leave it alone.'

I looked around at the sneering face of the man who'd just come in. Any other time I'd have given him an argument. As it was I muttered feebly,

'Guess you're right.'

I left there and flagged a cab. He didn't like the look of me, but cheered up when I told him to take me to Parkside. People over there don't go in too much for roughing up hackies.

Frank, the day-man, was still on duty, as I shambled up the steps.

'You O.K. Mr. Preston? You look like the Day of Judgement.'

'I'm all right, Frank. Thanks.'

'Cab, huh? What happened to the car? Say, that must be it. Been in some accident, right?'

'Right.'

'Well, just so you're O.K. You're better off than them gangsters, at that.'

'Gangsters?'

'Over to the del Pacifico. A bomb, they said on the radio. These two guys got blown to hell and gone. Right out there on the street. Terrible ain't it? I mean, innocent people could have got hurt.'

I thought of the blond boy and his friend.

'Terrible,' I agreed.

'Still, just so they only kill each other, I say.'

'That's right, Frank.'

Upstairs, I stood under the shower, letting the spray cut away the heat and the sweat and the dust. Letting it wash away that extra, secret odour that only fear produces. Drowsiness was beginning to get the better of me. What a man really needed was to stretch out on something comfortable, and let the world try to carry on without him for a few hours. Then I watched in irritation as my own hand reached out to the heat control. Icy water banged at the top of my skull, and coursed all over me, chasing away all thoughts of sleep. How can a man sleep when he's freezing to death? I made myself stand there until I was chilled to the marrow. Then I climbed out, with shivering limbs, and teeth to match.

A large rough towel felt good as I applied it violently all over. Sleep, nothing. What a man really needed was a drink — no, make that coffee. That was it. Coffee and a cigarette, the two best aids to clear thinking.

My first piece of clear thinking was to remember I hadn't spoken to Heather Dentman for hours. She'd be sitting there, waiting for a call. At least, she was supposed to be.

As soon as I was dressed, I dialled the number. It was several seconds before her voice replied.

'Yes?'

She sounded nervous, and slightly out of breath, both at the same time.

'Heather? Preston.'

'Oh, thank God it's you. Where've you been? I've been going frantic sitting here.'

'Sorry about that. Hither and yon is

where I've been. Did anyone call?'

'Not what we were expecting. I've had Cecile on the phone, though. My mother-in-law, that is.'

'I remember,' I told her drily. 'What did she want?'

'She wants me to go out there. Out to the house. Tonight. She says it's very important that she sees me right away.'

When Cecile Dentman makes up her mind about something, I reflected, she is not a lady to waste any time. She probably had Heather's plane ticket waiting on the hall table.

'What did you tell her?'

'I told her I wasn't sure. I was expecting a call. She didn't seem too pleased. Said she'd expect me.'

'We'll decide all that, later. Right now, I don't want you to say anything at all. Pack a few things, just enough for overnight, and get on over here to my place. You have the address.'

Pause.

'If this is what it sounds like — ', she began.

'I realised the way it must sound, even

as I was saying it,' I laughed. 'But that isn't the idea at all. The idea is I want you out of that apartment. Tonight.'

'But where will I go?' She was beginning to sound frightened.

'I'll arrange all that. But I don't want to talk on the phone. As it is, Hackett has quite enough to tell Cecile. Right, Hackett?'

I hoped I wasn't talking just for Heather's benefit.

'Hackett?' she repeated. 'I don't know what you're saying. You mean Mr. Hackett, the manager here?'

'Your lovely manager is probably listening to every word. Even if he isn't at the moment, it'll be on tape for when he's ready.'

'Oh,' she oh-ed. 'I don't know what to say.'

'Say nothing,' I advised. 'Just pack the stuff and come over. Thirty minutes?'

She made up her mind.

'Twenty,' she announced.

'Great. I'll see you then. And Heather, bring your own car. Mine is out of order.'

As I put down the phone, I wondered

what it was I was up to. So far as I was aware, Heather was in no danger. And yet there was that indefinable crawling feeling around the back of my neck that said in some way she'd be better off where I could keep an eye on her. Maybe I was making too much of it. Maybe I just wanted her around. She was one lady a man could very quickly get used to having around.

To pass the time, I spread newspaper on a table, and set about cleaning the Police Special. Soon, the parts were spread out gleaming dully with oil. Rourke would have been proud of me. While I was about it, I decided to give the little .28 a birthday as well. Rourke wouldn't have been so happy about that one, because I've never got around to reporting ownership. I took it away from somebody once, during a discussion we were having about some missing bonds. It's been useful on occasions, when a second gun has not been expected, but the dirt on the cleaning rag pointed out that it hadn't been put to work for a long time.

When the bell sounded, I wiped my hands, and went to the door.

'Who is it?'

'It's me, Heather.'

I opened up, and looked at her. Beautiful as always, but looking just a little less assured than usual. Maybe it had something to do with the small soft-leather grip she carried. We smiled at each other. I stood aside to let her in. Feet sounded quickly in the hallway. Heather was half inside, and turned, startled.

A man stood behind her, wearing the same friendly grin as when I last saw him in Clive Barnes' house. A man I now knew to be Pete 'Bright-Eyes' Hooper. In his hand was a large Luger.

'It's a party,' he announced. 'Let's all go in.'

Where I come from, the man with the Luger does the talking.

We all went in.

13

Hooper shut the door, and stood with his back against it, checking around with his eyes.

'Well now, this is nice,' he said chattily. 'Go on in Miss. Stand over by that table for a minute. You, Preston, bring that chair over here by the door.'

The man was all tensed up. He looked like hell. No shave, rumpled shirt, a lot of the surface good humour stripped away from him. I was looking at the man underneath now, the man in the police records, the one with a gun.

I carried the light chair over to where he was standing. He moved to one side, keeping well clear of me.

'Put it against the door,' he ordered.

I set it down, wondering.

'Now, sit in it.'

That made sense. It put me out of the action. There was nothing I could reach from there. Nothing to grab or throw. I was no danger to him. When I didn't sit immediately, he wagged the Luger with impatience. That made up my mind.

'O.K. Now you, lady. Over there oughta do it.'

He pointed to another chair. It was in a corner, and once there, Heather couldn't make any moves either. I was curious to know what came next. It looked to me as though the man wanted to talk. Right on cue, he said,

'That's nice. Now, we talk. Cigarettes?'

'Behind you.'

He found the pack, and lit an Old Favorite with evident satisfaction.

'I been hanging around out there, trying to figure a way to get in without making like a marine invasion,' he informed me.

'You could always knock on the door,' I reminded him.

He'd seen the dismantled hardware now, and stood looking down at it.

'Not many guys got enough brains to know about keeping their little pals clean,' he observed with approval. 'They think the damn things just go on shooting forever. I knew you was a guy to watch out for. I told Manny. I said, that guy ain't no furniture salesman. Told him that.'

'Poor old Manny. What did you guys quarrel about?'

'Quarrel? We didn't have no quarrel,' he looked mystified.

I shifted in the chair.

'Oh? I thought you must have had some kind of reason for knocking off your partners.'

He went pale, and his face twitched.

'You shut up talking that way, or somebody is really going to get knocked off around here.'

Heather had been listening to all this with wide eyes.

'Mark, what is this all about? Who is this man?'

She was scared, with reason, but the tone was controlled. I tried to keep emphasis from my voice, but the message had emphasis enough.

'His name is Hooper. Better do what he says, honey. People have a habit of dying around Mr. Hooper. He was at the

house with two other men when I found
Barnes' body. Now, today, those two men
died as well. In a fire. So we do whatever
he wants us to do. A couple of bodies, one
way or the other, won't make Mr. Hooper
lose any sleep.'

'You talk crazy,' he repeated. 'I had you
figured for a piece of the action, until they
tried to blow you up, over there at the
hotel tonight.'

My surprise was genuine.

'You saw that?' I demanded. 'A real
Chicago trick. You're from Chicago, right?
Are you telling me you weren't respon-
sible?'

'You talk crazy,' he repeated. 'I was just
following you around. Thought I might
learn something.'

My mind was roaring off in all
directions, and still not coming up with
answers.

'Following me?'

'Sure. After what happened to Shortie,
and Manny Levers, you was all I had. I
got my orders. If I go back home with
nothing, they'll tear my ears off. Just for
openers. You better start with the words,

Preston. Where do you figure in all this?'

Heather looked across anxiously. I'd have patted her hand, except she was ten feet away.

'I'm going to have to tell him,' I told her gently. 'Just trust me. This man is not interested in blackmail, believe me.'

She nodded tremulously, wanting to believe me.

'Blackmail? What's this about black-mail?'

I told him. About Barnes, about the letters, about the way Heather's mother-in-law felt about scandal. I told him all of it.

'Is that the truth, lady?'

He looked at her fiercely. Heather lowered her eyes, and her voice was small.

'Yes. I'm afraid it is.'

Hooper snorted in frustration, and took another cigarette.

'You oughta have more brains, a classy doll like you. You oughta get your head examined.' Then turning to me he said,

'None of this stuff is any use to me. If it's true, that is. Now tell me this, Mr. Detective, if you're just fooling around looking for a bunch of letters, why would they try to knock you off? The way you tell it, you're not even a nuisance.'

He glowered at me, all dark suspicion.

'I don't know,' I told him, honestly. 'I don't even know who 'they' are. Maybe if you opened up a little. I've told you my end of it. What's yours?'

'Talk?' he said incredulously. 'Me? Sounds like everybody around here is crazy.'

But his voice carried little conviction. I kept on talking.

'You said yourself I was all you had. Maybe I do know something — no, I'm not holding out — but maybe I know something important, without knowing I know it. If I heard your end of things, we might both find out what it is.'

His thumb made a rasping sound as he dragged it across the day's beard.

'I don't know,' he doubted.

'Look, I think we're running two different pictures here. We're in one picture, the lady and me, you're in a different one entirely. We have to find out where they join up. What can you lose?'

'Lose?' he echoed sourly. 'What can I lose, he says. I'll tell you. My life. That's what I can lose, if I louse this up. There's three guys dead here. That leaves me to do something about it.'

'Three?' interjected Heather. 'Are you saying Clive was one of these — these people? I won't believe it. I don't even know whether he ever saw Chicago.'

'No, Heather. The third man wasn't Clive. It was the man I told you about, named Earl Gannon. Am I right, Hooper?'

'How d'ya know that?' he countered.

'The police told me,' I replied. 'The gun that killed Barnes was the same one used on Gannon. They even thought I did it.'

'Cops,' he snorted. 'Dumb cops.'

'Not always. Gannon was married to Barnes' sister. They had a fight, and she left him. I think he came here to Monkton City to find out if Barnes knew where she was hiding. Am I right?'

'That's the way I got told.'

'So we have two suspects for Gannon's death. Barnes himself, and the sister. But they won't do. Barnes is out, because he didn't kill himself. The sister is out, because she'd had no reason to kill her own brother, even if she lost her temper with Gannon.'

Hooper was only half-listening. Now he snorted.

'You're really chasing your tail. Them civilians didn't have nothing to do with this.'

'But Barnes is dead,' I pointed out.

'He ran out of luck, is all. They had to kill him, the same way they have to get to you. He could put the finger on them, you see. Even if he didn't know it.'

The same as me. I didn't like that.

'That makes Barnes a very unlucky man,' I said. 'Me too, the way you tell it. Problem is, I still don't know why. It's no use waving that thing at me, Hooper. I repeat, I still don't know which way is up. But this much I know. If you're telling the truth, then you don't have a thing against me. I've done you no harm, and I couldn't even be a witness against you, on any charge. The way you tell this story, you didn't do anything.'

He didn't like it, I could tell that. He wasn't too strong in the think department, and what I had said was compelling him to think. While he was still working on it, I added,

'And this young lady is not involved anywhere at all. Why don't you just let her go home? We can settle this without her, one way or the other.'

But he wasn't going to stand for that.

'No,' he stated. 'The dame stays. It's bad luck for her, and she don't seem to figure anywhere in this, but that's too bad. She's seen me, knows who I am. That puts her in it.'

'I wish you'd both stop talking about me as though I wasn't here,' Heather cut in, suddenly annoyed out of her fear. 'You're like a couple of old women, with your suspicions about who knows what. You're the one with the gun, Mr. Hooper, it seems to me you should be more decisive.'

'Howsat?' he queried.

'Decisive,' I informed him. 'It means — '

'You shuddup. I know what it means.' He was watching Heather with a puzzled face. 'What way should I be more — decisive?'

'It's very simple. I know nothing at all. Mr. Preston has told you all he knows — oh yes, he has, I can vouch for that. The next step is for you to say what you know. Pool the information. After that, if we can't help you, either you go away, or —'

She shrugged. Hooper shook his head.

'You didn't finish, lady. Or what?'

'I would have thought it was obvious. Simple logic. You kill us both.'

I squirmed mentally, and wished she wouldn't talk that way. Hooper loved it. That wide, happy smile came back over his face.

'I'm sorry I called you a chump just now. That's a good head you got on them shoulders. You don't scare easy, do you lady?'

Ignoring the question, she gazed at him with level eyes.

'Well, what's the answer?'

'O.K.' he decided, 'I'll tell you what I know. It's kind of a long story. I wasn't nothing but a runt when it started. Still

235

busting open juke boxes, that kind of stuff. One day there's a big rumpus. It even gets down to little squirts like me, in case we knew anything. One of the top men had taken a powder. One of the real inside cash men. Just helped himself to the dough, bumped off two of the carriers, and melted away. The same night, the top lady in the girl business disappeared, with all the cash from that operation. There was a lot of noise at the time. These two were real inside people, none of your punks. It shook up the whole organisation for months.'

I could imagine. One of the biggest fears the syndicate has to live with is the possibility of one of its own inner counsellors going bad. One of the decision makers.

'What was the take?' I asked.

'Nobody ever knew for sure. You know how it is, you got numbers' money, track money, girl money, protection, it's all cash. Fives, tens, twenties. All kinds of money. People said there was fifteen million, thirty million, you know the way people go on. A story don't lose nothing in the telling, not a money story.'

'But you must have some idea.'

He nodded.

'After a while, when the big shock waves stopped coming, we heard a different yarn. Near as anyone could figure, there was somewhere between six and seven million dollars.'

I pursed my lips in a soft whistle.

'But every gun in the country would be out looking for a piece of that.'

'Right. This kind of stuff gets pulled every now and then. I guess it always will where there's cash. But usually it's some punk. He grabs twenty or thirty thousand plus the nearest good-looking dame. They head for the coast, book into the plushest hotel, start filling up the joint with champagne. If they get lucky, it might take four days before they're found. Then a couple of bodies get washed up on the beach, and it's all over.'

'Only this time was different,' I supplemented.

'You could say that,' he agreed. 'This time it wasn't no hell-raiser pushing off with some dumb hash-slinger. This was a real big man, a name, and as for the woman — well, I tell you, I may have been just a runt, but even I couldn't believe it.'

'The woman?' I prompted.

'She was top lady. A real society dame, I always heard. Not some ordinary madam. She ran the champagne end of the market, the real big stuff. Like for the politicians, and the big business guys. What's that word, diplomats, yeah, guys like that. They called her the Satin Lady, and she was something. They both were. Nobody could ever have figured them to pull a stunt like that.'

'For six million dollars, people will do a lot of things,' I reminded.

'Not syndicate people. Not if they got any brains. We have guys who specialise in brains. Like spreading 'em out on the sidewalk.'

Heather shuddered. I knew how she felt.

'So all this happened a long time ago? I gather, from what you say, that these two didn't book the honeymoon suite and start whooping it up?'

'Not them. They disappeared down a hole in the ground. Tell you the truth, I never even gave either of them a thought in years. Then, last week, Gannon comes out here to California. His wife took a powder, and he thinks maybe this brother will know where she's at. Gannon works for Manny Levers. We all do. We all did, I oughta say. Well, he phones up Manny, all excited. Guess who he thinks he seen, he says? Delano, that's who. He can't be sure, it's been a long time. People change.'

'Delano?' I butted in. 'That's the mobster who disappeared?'

'Mobster?' said Hooper disdainfully. 'That's a dirty word you got there. He wasn't no mobster. This is an important man we're talking about. Anyway, Gannon wants the boss to get him a picture of the guy. Send it out to him, so he can check it out better. Before that happens, we get the buzz. Somebody took a dislike to old Earl, and shot him full of holes.'

'Could have been the wife?' I suggested.

'Yeah,' he agreed. 'That's what I figured. But Manny hadn't told me about the phone call. Not then. After Earl got burned, he told us the yarn. Had to come check himself. And seeing what happened to Gannon, he wasn't going to come out here by himself.'

'And you thought Clive Barnes might provide the link, even if he wasn't aware of it.'

He shrugged.

'Right. All we knew was Barnes. When we got to his joint, somebody already scragged him. Then you showed up. You know what happened then.'

I scowled, rubbing at my head.

'I certainly do. Tell me, why did Levers play it that way? He could have slugged me before you went. Any of you could. Why go through the circus of leaving the house, and then having somebody bang me on the head from behind?'

'Slug you? From behind?'

Astonishment was written all over his face.

'You wanta feel the lump?'

'No, I don't, and you stay right in that

240

chair,' he scowled. 'You're telling me you got knocked out in that house? Who could've done it? It wasn't none of us.'

Realisation came to him. I nodded at the same moment.

'Right. I think we both know what happened. Whoever killed Barnes was still there. He must've been about to leave, when you three showed. Hid somewhere, deciding what to do. After you left, there was only me between him and the door.'

'Imagine,' breathed Hooper. 'We was that close. I guess you didn't get a look at him, huh?'

'No,' I affirmed. 'Maybe you could arrange that now?'

'Huh?'

'The photograph. You were supposed to bring a photograph of this Delano. Or did that go in the fire?'

'No. I got one in my pocket. We all had one. Here.'

Fishing in his pocket, he took out a shiny postcard-size picture. Walking across, he held it out for me to see. I looked at the smiling, confident face.

'Show it to the lady,' I suggested.

He stepped over, and held out the picture for Heather. She gave a small gasp.

'Why that's — '

'Yes it is,' I stopped her. 'And there's no doubt about it. O.K. Pete, you can put the gun away. The game is over.'

I got up from the chair. He made a threatening move, but I wagged my head.

'Stop wasting everybody's time. Think about money. I imagine there's a lot of money riding on this one?'

He lowered the gun, with evident reluctance.

'One hundred G's minimum. That's what they say. Could be more.'

'Well, that's a nice round sum. Maybe we'll cut you in for a few bucks.'

'Cut me in,' he exploded. 'Cut me in, he says. Listen, I am in. This is all mine, now. I'm the only one left. You talk to me nice, maybe I'll cut you in.'

I waved a patient hand at him.

'Wild talk, Pete. All you have is a photograph. You don't have a man to go with it. Without us, you have nothing. Think it over, but don't take too long.

You're down for one third of the profits.'

'One third? Listen — '

Again I interrupted.

'Work it out. Like in school. Which is better, one third of one hundred grand, or one hundred per cent of nothing? You can stretch your legs now, Heather. The nasty man doesn't want to kill us any more.'

She nodded uncertainly, licked her lips, and stood up. Pete Hooper paid her no attention. He was working out problems. Heather looked at each of us in turn, wondering what the next move was to be.

'Well?'

I walked to the table and began to fit the .38 back together. Hooper started to say something, shrugged, and stuck his own gun back in a pocket.

'Mr. Hooper and I are going visiting, honey. No, you're not invited. Neither are we, for that matter, so there's no telling what reception we'll get. I'll need your car, please. When we've gone, I want you to wait exactly fifteen minutes. Then call homicide. Be sure and talk to one of three people. The names are Rourke, Randall, Stratfold. You got that?'

'Rourke, Randall, Stratford,' she intoned.

'Stratfold,' I corrected, 'with an 'l'. Tell them where we've gone, tell them I'd appreciate some company out there. And make a point of saying we were armed when we left. They'll know what you mean. O.K.?'

'Why fifteen minutes?' she queried. 'Why not call right away?'

'That gives us a quarter hour at the house. It'll be more than enough. I have to protect you, me, and old George too. Plus, I have to give Mr. Hooper time to get away. If he needs it, that is.'

Hooper had been paying close attention.

'I don't like the part about the cops,' he objected. 'I don't need cops.'

'I'm sure you don't,' I agreed. 'But I do. Things might get a little rough where we're going. If there's an argument, I think we ought to come out best. But if that happens, you might get to thinking. You might think for instance, now that I started you on all that mental arithmetic, that three-thirds of one hundred thousand dollars is better than one-third.

I wouldn't want you to get the impression I don't trust you Pete, but the fact is, I don't trust you.'

'That goes double,' he growled.

Heather came over and put a hand gently on my arm.

'Mark, I don't pretend to understand half of what's going on,' she said softly. 'It never entered my head that this kind of thing might happen. There's no reason you should go risking your life. Nothing is that important.'

'It all got too big, too fast,' I explained. 'I'm in it now, like it or not. And besides, these people tried to kill me tonight. That makes it personal. Now, you're to stay here until I come for you, or call you on the phone. Nobody comes in. Nobody.'

'Very well.'

Hooper was getting more fidgety by the second.

'C'm on, c'm on, let's go, here' he snapped.

I squeezed Heather's hand.

'Fifteen minutes,' I reminded.

14

It took twenty-five minutes to drive out to the house. Pete Hooper sat hunched beside me, deep in his own thoughts. At one point he said,

'How do I know you won't feed me to the cops?'

I made a face in the darkness.

'You're not thinking, Pete. There's no reward out for these people. The only parties willing to pay any money are the mob. They won't pay me a red cent if I turn you in. More likely blow my head off some dark night. You don't have to trust me for my honest blue eyes. I need you alive before I can collect.'

'Ah.' He breathed deeply, satisfied now. People can always understand better when the map is illustrated with dollar signs.

The house was set well back from the road. There were lights at ground level, the upper half was in darkness. I cut the lights and switched off the motor.

'We'll walk up,' I said. 'Let's try to keep it quiet.'

He nodded, and we both climbed out, clicking doors gently shut. The gravel path would have been as discreet as a brass band. We walked on lawn, then on a flower bed leading to the side of the front door. Parked outside was a Toyota sedan, the one I'd seen outside Barnes' house, and assumed to belong there.

We took out our guns and edged silently along the verandah, to where light spilled into the night from open French doors. I eased one eye around the wall.

It was a peaceful scene. They sat watching television, drinks before them on a low glass table. I motioned Hooper to remain where he was, and keep quiet. He nodded understanding. I dropped the .38 into a side pocket, still holding it. Then I stepped into the room.

'Evening,' I said conversationally.

They both looked round, startled.

Cecile Dentman was the first to speak. I knew she would be.

'Preston,' she gasped. 'But you're
— you're — '

'Dead?' I supplied. 'No. Old Francesco
there ran out of luck on that one. He
killed a couple of kids not long out of
school.'

Mr. Dee was shocked with disbelief.
Just kept staring at me, and shaking his
head.

'Frank?' queried Cecile, standing up
and tossing her splendid head. 'Why, you
must be out of your mind. Why on earth
would Frank want to harm anyone? And
how dare you come bursting in here?'

She wore a floor-length houserobe of
Chinese patterned silk. The picture could
have been a full-page ad. in Harper's. I
grinned.

'You're a knockout, Cecile. All ways.
Appearance, style, voice. The whole
works. I'm not too sure about the robe,
though. Silk, isn't it? Is that correct dress
for the Satin Lady?'

* * *

A slim hand shot up to her throat in momentary agitation. Frank Dee lumbered to his feet, cursing.

'I wouldn't try anything, Delano,' I advised. 'That stunt with the bomb has made you something I don't care for too well. Be a real pleasure to smear you all over the wall.'

He stopped, in mid-stride towards me.

'Stop it, both of you,' commanded Cecile. 'This is a time for talk, not childishness. I'm sure there's nothing here we can't straighten out, if we use a little common sense.'

She actually stopped us. Dee, or I should say Delano, and I were squaring off at each other like two bulls in a field. And Cecile Dentman's voice stopped us.

'Now, let's all be sensible, and decide what we're going to do. To start with, let me get you a drink, Preston. I always think people should talk business over a drink.'

I watched in admiring amazement as she walked across to a side cabinet.

'Is scotch all right?'

I nodded, without speaking. My eyes

weren't really on her in any case. It doesn't pay to take your eyes off a man like Delano.

Silken arms reached out towards the crystal decanters. The turning round was smooth and swift, like an enraged tigress. Vaguely, I saw the nickel-plated automatic lining up on my middle. There was an explosion, and Cecile Dentman was smashed back into the cabinet, showering bottles and glasses as she went, clutching a ruined shoulder as the gun dropped from nerveless fingers.

Delano reacted instantly, diving away from me to where the automatic lay on the carpet. At that same time, I pulled the thirty eight free of my pocket, just as Hooper stepped inside, still covering the ashen-faced Cecile.

'Better pick it up, Frank,' I advised. 'I'm going to kill you anyway.'

He made up his mind, rolling over, the gun now in his hand. I saw the smiling face of the blond kid in the car. Then I shot him.

'That's enough.'

Hooper tapped me on the shoulder.

Some of the red drained away from my eyes. Delano was grasping at a ruined knee and cursing loudly.

'You ain't thinking,' advised Hooper. 'Dead, he's just another dead guy. Could be anybody. Alive, he's Frankie Delano, it can be proved. My people will only pay for Delano.'

It was so out of place it was almost funny. No appeal to humanity, no plea for mercy. Just dollar and cent logic. The only kind of thinking that Hooper could bring to bear on the question of whether a man should live or die.

My laugh was very close to hysterical. I managed to control myself, as Hooper bent down to retrieve the automatic.

'Handkerchief,' I snapped.

He stopped, puzzled, then nodded as he understood.

'Prints, right?'

'Right. They both handled that thing.'

'Yeah.' He knelt down, picking up the shining weapon with care. 'It's too bad they didn't take a shot at one of us. This way, things don't look so good.'

'Could I have a glass of water?' Cecile

moaned faintly between clenched teeth.

'Leave her alone,' I ordered. 'She won't die of thirst. Just don't get near her, and don't give her anything. And pass me that automatic.'

Pete Hooper gave her an apologetic shrug, and did as I asked. I took it with great care, wrapped in several thicknesses of handkerchief so the incriminating fingerprints were not smudged.

Then I went to the open window and pointed the gun out into the night. The two slugs I fired sped harmlessly into the darkness.

'Now they shot at us,' I explained. 'Her first. She fired at you. You had to shoot back. He grabbed the gun and tried for me. O.K.?'

'If I was a cop, I wouldn't like it,' he grumbled.

'They don't have to like it,' I pointed out. 'They can't prove anything different.'

'These two will tell it different,' he persisted.

I looked at the bleeding pair. Cecile was losing a lot of blood, and the colour was going from her face. Delano was already a dirty grey.

'What they say doesn't matter a damn. They can hire all the lawyers in the state, if they want. Who knows, maybe they'll even get away with it. It won't matter. They're both dead, right this minute. As soon as your boys in Chicago are satisfied about their identities, they'll be dead in hours.'

'One million,' gritted Cecile. 'Get us out of here, and I will give you one million dollars. Negotiable bonds.'

Hooper snorted before I did.

'One million? What's wrong with two? Or ten? I don't think you have the picture, lady. They ain't printed the kind of money can keep you safe from my people. What would I do with your million? Except maybe line my coffin with it.'

'He's right, Cecile,' I confirmed. 'As of now, your money is no good any more.'

Even through the pain, there was mocking in her eyes. Cecile Dentman was alive and wealthy. She wasn't through yet, her gaze told me. So far the world had done what she wanted. This was a setback, a big one, but it wasn't the end. She wouldn't be through until they shovelled the earth down on top of the big box.

Headlights pierced the outside night. There was a confusion of slamming doors, running feet, hoarse instructions. I winked at Hooper. From now on, it would be all cops.

★　★　★

I never did get my cut of the hundred thousand. A smooth looking corporation lawyer called to see me. Mr. Hooper had been mistaken, quite mistaken. All the people interested in tracing their old — um — business associates had long since retired or died. However, he quite understood that I had been put to some — er — inconvenience, and his clients were prepared to reimburse me for my trouble.

When he left, I was holding a check for one thousand dollars. My personal island in the South Pacific would have to be postponed for a while.

I never found out the truth about the letters Heather Dentman wrote, either. I always figured it was Charlie, the locker-room attendant out at the Bay End Club. He denied it, and there weren't any more blackmail threats, so it didn't seem to matter any more. I only saw Heather one more time. I asked her what she'd do next.

'I don't know,' she shrugged. 'After this terrible trial is over, maybe George and I will move away. Try again, perhaps. Who knows?'

I asked if I could call her for dinner sometime. She smiled ruefully.

'Thank you for asking, but no. This has all been a nightmare, an absolute nightmare. Please try not to misunderstand, but you would bring it all back. Keep it alive. I have to forget, or go crazy. You do understand don't you? It's nothing personal.'

I said oh sure I understood, and went away.

I'd been slugged, threatened, somebody tried to blow me up with a bomb. But it had all been in the way of business. It was nothing personal.

After a while I remembered Janie, the miniature hat-check girl at Annie Domino's. Now there was a chunk of unfinished business. Full of confidence, I breezed into the place one balmy evening. A succulent blonde looked me over with reserved approval.

'Good evening, sir,' she greeted.

'Hallo,' I replied. 'Where's little Janie? Night off?'

It would be just my luck to pick the one evening she didn't have to work.

'Why no. Janie isn't with us any longer. Haven't you heard?'

'Heard what?'

'Well,' she leaned confidentially across the counter. 'About her and Mr. Bronowitz. You know, the manager.'

I nodded, to show I'd heard the name.

'They ran off and got married. Right after we closed, the other night. Drove all night into Nevada, and got hitched. Isn't it romantic?'

'Swell,' I said flatly. 'Just great.'

The disappointment in my voice intrigued Blondie. Her eyes were full of

mischief as she said,

'Could I pass on a message?'

'No thanks. No message.'

Her voice throbbing with hopeful concern she asked,

'Was it something important? Something personal?'

I shook my head and made for the door.

'Nothing personal.'

YOU'RE BETTER OFF DEAD
NO GOLD WHEN YOU GO
MURDER IS FOR KEEPS
THIS'LL KILL YOU
NOBODY LIVES FOREVER

We do hope that you have enjoyed reading this large print book.

Did you know that all of our titles are available for purchase?

We publish a wide range of high quality large print books including:
**Romances, Mysteries, Classics
General Fiction
Non Fiction and Westerns**

Special interest titles available in large print are:
**The Little Oxford Dictionary
Music Book, Song Book
Hymn Book, Service Book**

Also available from us courtesy of Oxford University Press:
**Young Readers' Dictionary
(large print edition)
Young Readers' Thesaurus
(large print edition)**

For further information or a free brochure, please contact us at:
**Ulverscroft Large Print Books Ltd.,
The Green, Bradgate Road, Anstey,
Leicester, LE7 7FU, England.
Tel:** (00 44) 0116 236 4325
Fax: (00 44) 0116 234 0205

Other titles in the
Linford Mystery Library:

DEATH SQUAD

Basil Copper

Lost in a fog on National Forest terrain, Mike Faraday, the laconic L.A. private investigator, hears shots. A dying man staggers out of the bushes. Paul Dorn, a brilliant criminal lawyer, is quite dead when Mike gets to him. So how could he be killed again in a police shoot-out in L.A. the same night? The terrifying mystery into which Faraday is plunged convinces him that a police death squad is involved. The problem is solved only in the final, lethal shoot-out.

DEAD RECKONING

George Douglas

After a large-scale post office robbery, expert Peterman Edgar Mulley's fingerprints are found on a safe and he lands in jail. The money has never been recovered, and three years later Mulley makes a successful break for freedom. The North Central Regional Crime Squad lands the case when a 'grasser' gets information to them. But before Chief Superintendent Hallam and Inspector 'Jack' Spratt can interrogate the informer, he is found dead. Then, a second mysterious death occurs . . .

THE SILENT INFORMER

P. A. Foxall

A man found murdered in a quiet street brings the police a crop of unpleasant problems. But when the victim is found to have a criminal record, an affluent lifestyle, and no visible honest means of support, the problems proliferate. It seems there could be a lot of villains who wanted him dead. The Catford detectives suddenly find themselves immersed in new enquiries into apparently unrelated crimes of two years ago, which can now be seen to add up to a murderous conspiracy.

DEATH THROWS NO SHADOW

Leo Grex

Mike Capper, a Fleet Street freelance, is after Baroness Rorthy's incredible personal story. However, after making a surprise rendezvous with her, he finds himself confronted by the notorious Andy Beecham, whose Casino Palace is London's latest fashionable fun-spot. Chief Superintendent Gary Bull and Inspector Bert Whitelaw are brought into a mystery which is attended by menace and murder. They uncover a scheme by villains to make use of North Sea oil for a purpose not included in the oil men's plans.

DEAD WOOD

Brian Parvin

The mystery surrounding Peggy Dilke began on the night they found her body in the Fenland wildlife reserve; the night her father, the man they called King Tin, vowed he had known his daughter's return to Near Unthank would end in a death. But whose — the entrepreneur Dutchman, Van Geet; the embittered Tom Clifford, or was it King Tin's accountant, who shared the Dilke secret? Inspector Mole sifts the shadows of fate and a family's past for the truth.

MURDER IS RUBY RED

E. and M. A. Radford

William Coppock, a well-known jeweller, was found dead in his car which was half submerged in the River Thames at Henley. An inquest decided that he had died from misadventure. Two months later, for no reason at all except his legendary 'suspicious mind', Doctor Manson, Scotland Yard's homicide chief, had the body exhumed — and found murder; and a ring of remarkable frauds. It took journeys to Paris, Amsterdam and Burma to find clues which eventually solved the crime.